The Oedipus Legend

The tragic story of King Oedipus is one of the great dramas that Western culture has inherited from Ancient Greece. It has penetrated the literature, legend and language of all ages.

Towering above the gallery of characters that Sophocles created are two who stand as universal symbols of human nature in its frailty and strength: Oedipus, the king who unknowingly killed his father and married his mother and who atoned for these crimes by a voluntary act of self-punishment . . . and Antigone, his daughter who placed right and dignity above her life.

Here for the first time is a translation that renders the Theban plays into a contemporary English which brings the characters and story to life with all the power, all the emotion and all the feeling of the original Greek.

Also included are a glossary of classical names, notes on pronunciation and meter, suggestions for production and acting, and historical material, which offer the reader a greater appreciation of Sophocles' dramatic genius.

Professor Bernard M. W. Knox of the Department of Classics of Yale University said of this translation of *Oedipus the King:* "Direct and forceful." And the poet William Carlos Williams called this translation of *Antigone:* "Brilliantly successful . . . as spirited and powerful as the original must have been."

THE OEDIPUS PLAYS OF

Sophocles

>>>

OEDIPUS THE KING

OEDIPUS AT COLONUS

ANTIGONE

In a new translation by

PAUL ROCHE

A MENTOR BOOK

NEW AMERICAN LIBRARY

NEW YORK
PUBLISHED IN CANADA BY
PENGUIN BOOKS CANADA LIMITED, MARKHAM, ONTARIO

Library of Congress Catalog Card No. 58-12838

 MENTOR TRADEMARK REG. U.S. PAT. OFF. AND FOREIGN COUNTRIES
REGISTERED TRADEMARK—MARCA REGISTRADA
HECHO EN DRESDEN, TN. U.S.A.

SIGNET, SIGNET CLASSIC, MENTOR, ONYX, PLUME, MERIDIAN AND
NAL BOOKS are published *in the United States* by
NAL PENGUIN INC.,
1633 Broadway, New York, New York 10019,
in Canada by Penguin Books Canada Limited,
2801 John Street, Markham, Ontario L3R 1B4

32   33   34   35   36   37   38   39   40

PRINTED IN THE UNITED STATES OF AMERICA

ΣΟΦΟΚΛΕΟΥΣ ΑΝΤΙΓΟΝΗ

Ω ΚΟΙΝΟΝ ΑΥΤΑΔΕΛΦΟΝ ΙΣΜΗΝΗΣ ΚΑΡΑ
ΑΡΟΙΣΘΟΤΙ ΖΕΥΣ ΤΩΝ ΑΠ ΟΙΔΙΠΟΥ ΚΑΚΩΝ
ΟΠΟΙΟΝ ΟΥΧΙ ΝΩΝ ΕΤΙ ΖΩΣΑΙΝ ΤΕΛΕΙ
ΟΥΔΕΝ ΓΑΡ ΟΥΤ ΑΛΓΕΙΝΟΝ ΟΥΤ ΑΤΗΣ ΑΤΕΡ
ΟΥΤ ΑΙΣΧΡΟΝ ΟΥΤ ΑΤΙΜΟΝ ΕΣΘ ΟΠΟΙΟΝ ΟΥ
ΤΩΝ ΣΩΝ ΤΕ ΚΑΜΩΝ ΟΥΚ ΟΠΩΠ ΕΓΩ ΚΑΚΩΝ

Foreword

<<<<<<<<<<<<<<<<<<<<<<<<<<<<<<<<<<<<<<<<<<

THE GREAT ENCOUNTER

Sophocles, who died at the age of nearly ninety, two thousand three hundred and sixty-four years ago, was one of the world's greatest poets and dramatists, and he speaks to us today with a message no less necessary and elevating than it was to the Greeks of the fifth century B.C. We too need to be told that man is but a limited and contingent creature, subject to sudden disrupting forces. Success is not finally to be measured by fame or material prosperity. Human greatness consists ultimately in nobly accepting the responsibility of being what we are; human freedom, in the personal working out of our fate in terms appropriate to ourselves. Though we may be innocent, we are all potentially guilty, because of the germ of self-sufficiency and arrogance in our nature. We must remember always that we are only man and be modest in our own conceits. Our place in the total pattern of the cosmos is only finite. That is not to say that it may not be glorious. Whatever our circumstances, we can achieve and endure through to essential greatness. It is not what fate has in store for us that matters, but what we do with it when it comes. There may be suffering, but no abiding hopelessness. No power, no imposition, no catastrophe, can uproot the personal dignity of each human being. The seeming caprice and unfairness of life, striking some down and pampering others, is only the beginning of the Great Encounter. Both the choice and the destiny are ours.

Smith College   Paul Roche
Northampton
May 1, 1958

CONTENTS

Introduction

>>

THE THEBAN TRILOGY

The story of Oedipus King of Thebes, his success, his fall, his awed and hallowed end—in brief, the Theban Legend—was already old in the time of Sophocles. Perhaps it stood to the great poet and dramatist in something of the same light that the legend of King Arthur and the Holy Grail stood to the poet Tennyson: a legend celebrated by several hundred years of song and poetry.

But, whereas Tennyson looked back on a dreamlike world of chivalry, and helped to sustain the dream of courtly romance, Sophocles looked back on an elemental world of human frailty, pride and punishment, and helped to sustain the dreadful inevitability of a family moving towards catastrophe. The world of King Arthur seemed beautifully impossible and Tennyson left it so; the world of King Oedipus seemed thankfully improbable but Sophocles left it terrifyingly possible.

In each of the three plays that comprise his Theban Trilogy—*Oedipus the King, Oedipus at Colonus,* and the *Antigone*—Sophocles shows us a character pursued to and pursuing its end amid the full illusion both of freedom and of destiny and so to a gloriously headstrong doom. It is true that the downfall of the House of Oedipus was foretold by the gods even before Oedipus was born, but it was foretold because it was going to happen; it was not going to happen because it was foretold.

The tragedy of King Oedipus was not only that he suffered the improbabilities of murdering his father and marrying his mother—both were mistakes anyway—the tragedy was that having murdered his father and married his mother he made the fully responsible mistake of find-

◀◀

ing it out. As he was an upright man, but proud, the gods allowed him to make the first mistake; as he was a headstrong man, but overweening in self-confidence, he allowed himself to make the second. Zeal mysteriously worked with destiny to trip him up on his self-righteousness and then reveal an arrogance which pressed forward to calamity.

But even fallen pride need not remain prostrate. In the second play, the *Oedipus at Colonus,* we are shown an old man, blinded, beaten, hunted through the years, rise to a new dignity by the very fact of his being the recognized vehicle of divine justice. We now know the worst that can happen to man, but it can only happen through a foolish stepping outside from the stream of man's right relationship to God. Now we see Oedipus, by his magnanimous acceptance of Fate, step back again. He is both cursed and blessed, and a living testimony to the vindication of man through suffering: not of course suffering in the Christian sense—for the horror and recalcitrance are still there—but suffering in that it is a lesson, a proud and acknowledged testimony to the truth.

In the last play, the *Antigone,* Sophocles returns to the theme of the first and shows us again what happens when the ostensibly good man succumbs to pride. This time, however, there is an added poignancy: Creon, who is the protagonist rather than Antigone, and who is a kind of second Oedipus in his ruthless pursuit of what he thinks is right, brings final ruin to the House of Oedipus, destroying not only himself, his wife, his son, the love of these for him, but the very person his son is going to marry and the one who is most dedicated to the right—Antigone.

So must always be the end of man without God, even religious man—for both Oedipus and Creon thought that they were religious. The horror for us, as it was for the Greeks, is precisely to see that an Oedipus or a Creon can so easily be ourselves. Both display the glory and the weakness (the fatal flaw) of self-sufficient man. And when Oedipus, the once upright, is dragged piecemeal, by his own doing, from wealth and power, is stripped of reputation, made to wallow in a bed of murder, incest, suicide, even personal disfigurement, the audience passes through such territories of fear and pity that the human heart is altogether purged.

THE RE-CREATION

If it is true that dramatic poetry is the language of speech, but speech made perfect, and true that poetry gives to plot its feeling, then my aim in this new translation of Sophocles is to make that speech as real as possible without ever letting it cease to be poetry. The difficulty of doing this for Sophocles is that he was no ordinary poetic genius. All great poets can rise to an occasion; but Sophocles does not need an occasion: he achieves his magical effects at will. He makes the simplest words and phrases sound like the loftiest epic utterance, and he makes the loftiest epic utterance sound as natural as everyday speech. With Sophocles dramatic poetry is the language of speech made perfect and the perfection of language made speech.

Herein lies the challenge to the translator: after he has captured the sense of that perfect speech how does he proceed to capture the magic of its sound? For if poetry lies somewhere between meaning and music, sense and sound, it is obvious that when meanings cross the barrier of different tongues they do not take their music with them: they have to assume new sounds and these new sounds may not be the aesthetic equivalent of the original. This is true of any two languages. "La plume de ma tante" is obviously not the same as "My aunt's pen," though who shall say exactly where the difference lies?

We need not, however, go further than our own language to see that different sounds can have the same meaning and yet a quite dissimilar feeling. "Lamp" is not the aesthetic equivalent of "light," nor "daybreak" of "early morning." "Highroad" does not have the same feeling to it as "main road" nor "chair" as "seat." The differences here are subtle but they are there. Sometimes the differences are crude and obvious: no one (even in his cups) would get up from a meal saying: "Well, I've never had better cutlets of dead calf or swallowed mellower fermented grape juice."

It is, then, not merely differences of meaning that control differences of feeling, but also differences of sound. "Thou odoriferous stench, sound rottenness," is not at all the same as "You sweet smell, healthy decay," though who will say the meaning is different? "In Xanadu did Kubla Khan a stately pleasure dome decree" bears almost no emotional resemblance to, "Kubla Khan decided upon a fine fun dome in Xanadu." It is precisely these different values of sound that guide and indicate the changes of feeling in any language. It is the balance of sounds in an infinitely complex interplay of rhythms and cadences that creates all those shifting associations of meaning and feeling, those allusions, hints and half-meanings, that constitute the pattern of living speech.

This is what makes translating poetry so exacting. It is not merely meanings that a translator has to match but feelings, and for this there are no rules that he can follow —he can only depend upon his ear. And to do this he must be a poet. If he cannot tell that "my Italy" has not the same ring to it as "Italia mia," that "chez moi" is not quite the same as "home," and that the "alpha and the omega" is the same and yet utterly different from "A to Z," then he had better leave the business of translating poetry alone. He might possibly end up by rendering Tennyson's famous lines: "Break, break, break on thy cold grey stones O sea" into "Cassez-vous, cassez-vous, cassez-vous sur vos froids gris cailloux O mer,"* which would be equivalent aesthetically to someone's translating the glorious cry of Xenophon's Ten Thousand: "Thalassa! Thalassa!" (The Sea! The Sea!) into "A vast ex-

* I am indebted to Miss Edith Hamilton for this witty example.

panse of salt water! A vast expanse of salt water!" Perfectly accurate of course.

It does not do then in poetry to forget sound. All feeling is controlled by the shape of sounds—their differences of cadence and rhythm. It is not simply that different sounds have different meanings, but that the same meanings have different sounds. Words are unbelievably sensitive. And in poetry mere clarity has very little to do with feeling. An increase of clarity can even spell the end of feeling; for poetry being half music has the power of making itself felt long before it has made itself fully understood.

> I fled him down the nights and down the days,
> I fled him down the arches of the years . . .

can be made far more straightforward and clear (and valueless): "For many years I made great efforts to avoid him." The health has gone from it.

These things being so, I took it as my principle that the translator of poetry must never rest satisfied with simply rendering the correct meaning of the words. This is only half his duty. The other half is to search out and to organize from the paucity or the abundance of words in his own language those words which can conjure up a similar feeling. He must rework the original words into a new system of sounds and rhythms that are so true to the nuances of his own language that they might almost seem to have been first created in that language to express the original feelings. He must therefore be aware of the essential differences between his own language and the original and yet be able to see constant analogies between them. For it is only by relating the known to the less known that a transformation takes place. Re-creation, not imitation, is what is called for.

Suppose, for instance, that the translator of Sophocles decides to cast his lines in hexameters simply because the Greek trimeter is also a six-measured line. He will find at once that he has not got the aesthetic equivalent: the

Greek trimeter is light and quick, the English hexameter dawdles and hesitates.

Suppose he goes to the other extreme and far from trying to imitate the Greek he ignores it and casts his lines in English rhymed tetrameter. He may get lightness and speed all right but now he will have something as foreign in feeling to the original as *The Rime of the Ancient Mariner* is to the Book of Job.

The poet-translator, then, must keep his eyes and ears on each of the languages: never imitating the one but seizing every chance for a parallel effect with the other. Compared to Anglo-Saxon poetry Greek poetry is spare in metaphor but rich in sound. He must somehow resolve this difference so that the Greek sparsity of ornament does not come out in English as bald uninspiring sound. Compared to Anglo-Saxon poetry Greek poetry is often direct and primitive in emotion but condenses great complexity of expression in a single compound epithet: the translator must somehow contrive to find a bond between the two so that the Greek compressed simplicity does not come out in English as verbiage or naïveté.

The style of Shakespeare and the style of the King James Bible (pillars of English literary form) could not be more different in sensibility from the style of Sophocles, and yet the poet-translator must find some analogy between them if he is to make a bridge between the two sensibilities. Luckily, there *are* analogies, likenesses, parallel feelings, for the design of words and the beauty of sound. The two languages do in fact pay attention to a great many of the same things: there is a preoccupation with cadence, which shows itself in a love of alliteration and assonance and the associative power of similar sound; there is an attention to rhythm, which shows itself in (among other things) the well-timed pause, the break in the middle of the line; a love of antithesis of sound and sense: there is a feeling for the symmetrical phrase as well as the asymmetrical as a means to emphasis; the use of repetition and parallelisms of speech for pointing up a phrase or creating pathos; a predilection for twists of expression, telling paradoxes, oxymora, litotes, and a whole host of figures of speech that help to put salt on the tongue and tonic in the head. These are the powerful emotive devices that Greek shares with Anglo-Saxon. If a translator is deaf to them in the Greek he will be deaf to them in English and he will remain comparatively numb to the feelings they engender. It is just here, it seems to me, that the poet-translator has his chance of paralleling the force and beauty of the Greek without ever deserting the native genius of English. He will be respecting similarities without at the same time attempting to camouflage differences.

In my own efforts I have been careful to watch Sophocles. Where he has repeated a word I have repeated it; where he is rich in assonance and alliteration, I try to be; where he is harsh and staccato, I try to catch it; where he has a ringing tone, I try to ring.* I have tried to walk and to run, to rise and to sit, with the Master, but never by imitation, only by analogy, transposition, re-creation. In translation there has to be a change of instruments, but the tune, the feelings as relayed through sound, must remain as quiet, as excited, as sublime, as intense, as in the original.

Such is the challenge. The poet-translator has as his ideal the creation of a pattern of sound which gets so close to the feeling of the original that it goes beneath the barrier of language and time, and lays bare the original creations of the Master. We ought not to have to remind ourselves that Oedipus, Antigone, Creon, Jocasta and the other characters of Sophoclean tragedy were first conceived as human beings. They have not changed since. They are in fact universal and timeless and we ought primarily to see them that way rather than as Greek characters in a Greek period piece.

* The reverse of this, of course, is not necessarily true: if I have repeated a word, it may not always be that Sophocles has repeated it.

‹‹

The language of Sophocles is concentrated, vivid, spirited and powerful. Cardinal Newman calls it, "the sweet composure, the melodious fullness, the majesty and grace of Sophocles." But it was also free, molten, fusile with elements taken from the lofty poetry of the epic, the strains of the lyric, and the lowly commonplaces of the market square.* He was a careful craftsman but far from being a safety-first artist. Amazing agility and subtlety often consort with a quite conscious want of accuracy. He wrote in a Greek never quite heard before. He took risks with the language: coining words, inventing grammatical and syntactical constructions, condensing, eliding, twisting figures of speech inside out, and sometimes stretching the elasticity of the Greek language (that most lively of languages) to breaking point. But in the end, at least when it is given to the ear and not the eye alone to judge, he makes everything sound moderate, simple, and natural. In my efforts to follow him I have not scrupled to turn my back on the purely literary, the pedantic, and the circumspect in diction. I have used a language which I hope is contemporary but new, transcending if possible the mere aptness of a modern idiom. I daresay I have sometimes run the risk of looking 'not quite right,' but perhaps not more so than Sophocles himself might have looked to some of his contemporaries had they only seen his lines and never heard them. I have coined a construction here and there and, in the *Antigone*, a word, but always with only one end in view: a deepening of the fear, the pity, the love, the pathos, the hate, contained in the original. I have throughout thought more of the sequence of Sophocles' feelings and ideas than of the apparent grammatical connection of his words; remembering that Sophocles himself wrote at a time when the Greek language had not finally set. I have always asked myself not: is such and such a phrase rendered meta-

---

* There are echoes in Sophocles of the proverb, the cliché and (as far as we can tell) the colloquial phrase. I have not ostracized any of these where they have served dialogue and emotion.

>>

phrastically according to the book of grammar or, for that matte , according to the lexicon, but—is it true? Is it natural? Is it poetical and rhythmical? Is it dramatically convincing and expressive of the human heart?*

The choruses in Sophocles are swift, energetic, and moving, but they are not easy. I have not tried to make them easy. I should hope, however, to have made them evocative. Their function in the original (helped on by dance, spectacle, and song) was to bridge the gap between the audience and the players and to intensify the emotion. For this reason I have allowed myself a very full vocabulary; for I wanted the widest possible range of sound. There seemed no reason, for instance, in avoiding the emotionally right word simply because it happened to be unusual or of non-Anglo-Saxon origin.† There is a time for the simple and a time for the complex. The Sophoclean choruses in their tense and mobile harmony of shifting sounds had an effect more powerful than mere narration, more immediate than plot. There is a time for music and a time for reasoning.

The three plays that are given here are three of the only seven that have come down to us. Altogether, Sophocles wrote some hundred and twenty-five plays, but only a few fragments and the titles of some have survived.

---

* These are the questions that Lewis Campbell, one of the greatest Greek scholars of the last century, propounds to the would-be Sophoclean interpreter.

† There are also instances in the plays where I might seem to be using words of a too Christian connotation. For instance, Antigone is made to say, "I shall beg the saints below to judge me leniently . . . ," and in the same play the word "sacraments" is used. In both these and other instances I maintain that the anachronism is justified and that I need not sacrifice a genuine parallel effect of feeling for the sake of an exactitude. Indeed, I believe the Greek words in the context of Sophocles had for his contemporaries a feeling analogously equivalent to that which they have for us 'anno Domini.' If not, then we are in a bad way indeed, for ultimately at least half the words we use are not identical but only analogous replicas of their ancient counterparts. Only Nature (and things very close to her) maintains an everlastingly stable currency of exactly exchangeable terms.

‹‹

The last of the three in the Theban Trilogy, the *Antigone*, was written first and is sometimes said to be his thirty-second play in order of production. It probably belongs to his middle period and Sophocles must have been about fifty-five. The first of the three, *Oedipus the King*, was written some sixteen years later when Athens was at the height of her fame and power. The second play, *Oedipus at Colonus*, was written last—perhaps last of all his plays —when Sophocles was nearing ninety: an old man well-loved and still distinguished for his refinement, balance and nobility of mind, but perhaps a little disillusioned with life and ready to say good-bye to it. He had seen his sons rebel against him in court, and now was forced to see his darling Athens nearing the end of her death struggles with Sparta—bankrupt, tottering in the dust, her sacred olive groves cut down, and her springing fountains dry.

As did Sophocles, I attempted the *Antigone* first, and though I have not his advantage of being able to put some thirty-four years between it and the *Oedipus at Colonus* I have perhaps unwittingly reflected something of his advance as a poet from the wonderful, but less mature, artistry of the *Antigone* to the perfect smoothness, naturalness, and sublimity of his *Oedipus at Colonus*. No one of course would dare to suggest that the Greek of the *Antigone*, so strong and so beautiful, is not already perfect, but Sophocles himself might have thought so. Indeed, there is a pregnant phrase quoted by Plutarch in which Sophocles described his own development by saying that "after working off the Aeschylean grandiloquence of his earlier style, and then the artificiality and crudity of his own style, he thirdly arrived at one which was *most expressive of character and most perfect*."* Be that as it may, rough diamonds in any language have their own perfection and a too consistent sparkle can dim the eye to deeper beauties.

* ἠθικώτατον και βέλτιστον. I have taken this observation from *The Style of Sophocles* by Professor F. R. Earp (Cambridge, 1944), to whom I am greatly indebted for his illuminating analysis.

Oedipus the King

>>>

for DUNCAN GRANT

my choice and master
spirit of this age.

THE CHARACTERS

<<<<<<<<<<<<<<<<<<<<<<<<<<<<<<<<<<<<<<<<<<<<<<<

OEDIPUS: king of Thebes

A PRIEST of Zeus

CREON: brother of Jocasta

CHORUS of Theban Elders

TIRESIAS: a blind prophet

JOCASTA: wife of Oedipus

A MESSENGER from Corinth

A SHEPHERD

A PALACE OFFICIAL

Palace attendants

Citizens of Thebes

TIME AND SETTING

Some fifteen years previously, OEDIPUS, then a young man, was told by the Oracle at Delphi that he was destined to murder his father and marry his mother. Shocked, he determines never to go back to Corinth, where he was brought up by the king and queen, who he thinks are his father and mother. His wanderings bring him eventually to the city of Thebes, where his real father and mother reign. However, on the way, he brawls with an old man in a carriage over right of way and in a fit of temper kills him. Arrived at Thebes, he finds the city in an uproar: the king, LAIUS, has gone on a mysterious journey and never returned, and a female monster, the Sphinx, has taken up her position on a rock outside Thebes and is strangling the inhabitants one by one for not being able to answer her riddle. OEDIPUS answers it and the Sphinx throws herself from her rock. The citizens, in gratitude, make OEDIPUS their king and he marries JOCASTA, their widowed queen. No one knows that JOCASTA is OEDIPUS' real mother and that the old man he killed on the road was LAIUS, his father. Nor do they know that these parents of his had tried to murder him as a baby (because of another dreadful oracle), and thought they had succeeded. There follow fifteen years of apparent prosperity: a sham prosperity cloaking corruption. The gods are disgusted. Thebes is struck by plague. The people of the city, led by their priests and elders, flock around the great and successful OEDIPUS, now in the prime of life and power. He saved them once: he can save them again. Here the play begins.

It is midmorning outside the palace of OEDIPUS, with Thebes in the background. There is the sound of prayer and lamentation; the air is full of incense. A procession of children, youths, and elders, all holding olive branches wreathed in white wool, are marshaled by a priest onto the palace steps and group themselves around the altar of Zeus. OEDIPUS comes out of the palace. He signals for silence.

Oedipus the King

>>>

PROLOGUE

OEDIPUS: Children, children! Scions of the ancient
Cadmean line!
What is the meaning of this thronging round
my feet—
  this holding out of olive boughs all
wreathed in woe?
The city droops with elegiac sound
  and hymns with palls of incense hang.
I come to see it with my eyes, no messenger's.
Yes, I whom men call Oedipus the Great.

[He turns to the PRIEST*]*

Speak, Elder, you are senior here.
Say what this pleading means,
  what frightens you, what you beseech.
There's not a thing I could coldbloodedly
  refuse petitioners so pitiful.

PRIEST: King Oedipus, the sovereign of my land,
  you see here young and old clustered
round the shrine:
Fledglings some, essaying flight,
  and some much weighted down
  (as I by age, the Presbyter of Zeus),
  and striplings some—ambassadors of youth.
In the market place sit others too
  at Pallas' double altar, garlanded to pray;
  and at the shrine where Ismenus breathes
oracles of fire.

Yes, look upon the city, see the storm
 that batters down this city's prow in waves
    of blood.
The crops diseased, disease among the herds.
The ineffectual womb rotting with its fruit.
A fever-demon wastes the town
 and decimates with fire, stalking hated
 through the emptied house where Cadmus
    lived:
While poverty-stricken night grows fat
 on groans and elegies in Hades Halls.

We know you are no god, omnipotent with
    gods.

That is not why we throw ourselves
 before you here, these little suppliants
    and I.
It is because on life's unequal stage
 we see you leader of men and consummate
 atoner to the powers above.
      For it was you,
 coming to the Cadmus capital,
 who disenthralled us from the Sphinx—
    her greedy dues—
 that ruthless sorceress who sang.
Not primed by us, not taught by hidden lore,
 but helped by God—in no way else, we
    think—
 you raised us up again and made us sound.

So, Oedipus, you most respected king,
 we plead with you to find for us a cure:
Some answer blown from God or—could it
    be?—
 enlightenment from man. For, still I see
 the prowess of the well-proved mind—
 its tested buoyancy.
      So, holy Sovereign, go.
Raise up our city. Go. Now on your guard.
Your old devotion celebrates you still,

>>

"Defender of the State." You must not let
your reign go down as one when men
were resurrected once—and once relapsed.
Mend the city, make her safe.
You had good omens once. You did your
work.
Be equal to your stature now.
If king of men (as king you are),
then be it of a kingdom manned and not
a desert.
The ship is lost, the turret blind,
with crew and lookout gone.

OEDIPUS: Your news, poor earnest children, is not new
to me.
I know it well. You all are sick—yet sick,
not one so sick as I. Your pain
is single, each to each—it does not breed.
Mine is treble anguish crying out
for the city, for myself, for you.
It was no man asleep you woke—ah no!
But one in bitter tears and one
perplexed in thought, found wandering.
Who clutched the only remedy that came:
To send the son of Menoeceus, Creon—
my own Jocasta's brother—to the place
Apollo haunts at Pythia; to learn
what act or covenant of mine
could still redeem the state.
And now I am afraid.
I count the days. His time is up.
He does not come. He should be here.
But when he comes—the instant he arrives—
whatsoever he shall tell me from the god,
that to the hilt I must do—or I am dam-
nable.

PRIEST: Good words to hear! And timely words,
for, look: they're signaling that Creon
comes.

‹‹‹

[CREON *is seen approaching in the distance*]

OEDIPUS: His eyes are bright. O great Apollo
    bring him here all effulgent with success!

PRIEST: He has a lucky look, at least:
    Bay-laurel chaplets thick with berries on his
             head.

OEDIPUS: We shall see in a moment. He can hear us
             now.

[OEDIPUS *shouts to him*]

Royal brother, what news? What mandate,
    Son of Menoeceus, from the mouth of God?

[CREON *answers as he enters*]

CREON: Favorable! I'd even say our wounds,
    God's behest done, will issue into blessings.

OEDIPUS: Which means? . . . You leave me half in hope,
    half buried in despair.

CREON: Will you hear it publicly? I am ready.
    Or shall we go inside?

OEDIPUS: Speak out to all.
    It's more for them than me; though more my
             own
    than my own soul.

CREON: Very well, then: here is what the god has
             said.

The Prince Apollo openly enjoins on us
    to sever from the body politic
    a monstrous growth that battens there.
Stop feeding that which festers.

OEDIPUS: By what treatment? How prescribed,
    how diagnosed?

CREON: By banishment;
    or death for death. The city frets with
    someone's blood.

OEDIPUS: Whose? Is the unhappy man not named?

CREON: Laius, sire—him we had as king
          in days before you ruled.

OEDIPUS: So I've heard.
          A man I never saw.

CREON: A murdered man.
          And now clearly is required the just blood
          of his assassins.

OEDIPUS: And they could be
          anywhere on earth. O where discover
          trace or track of a faraway crime?

CREON: "Here," says the god. "Seek and you shall
                                              find.
          Only that escapes which never was pursued."

OEDIPUS: Where did Laius meet his violent death?
          At home? Abroad? In the fields?

CREON: He planned
          a pilgrimage, he said; and so left home;
          never to come back again the way he went.

OEDIPUS: He went alone? No companions and no wit-
                                              nesses
          who could furnish a report?

CREON: Dead. All done to death but one, who fled in
                                              panic;
          and he tongue-tied save on a single point.

OEDIPUS: What point? Tell it. Clues breed clues
          and we must snatch at straws.

CREON: This man
                                    insists
          that highwaymen attacked the King—not
                                              one
          but many. And they cut him down.

OEDIPUS: High-
                                    waymen!

<<<<<<<<<<<<<<<<<<<<<<<<<<<<<<<<<<<<<<<<<<<<<<<

   No highwayman would be so bold, unless
          . . . unless
    someone here put him up to it with bribes.

CREON: So we thought; but with Laius gone
    we were sunk in miseries and no one
          stirred—
   his death went unavenged.

OEDIPUS: What miseries
   could ever let you leave unsolved
   the death and downfall of a king?

CREON: Sir, it was the siren Sphinx of riddles,
   who sang us from the shadowed past
   to what was sorely present.

OEDIPUS: Then I'll go back and drag that shadowed
          past to light again.
   Oh yes, the pious Phoebus and your piety
   has set on foot a duty to the dead:
   A search which you and I together will
          pursue.
   My designs could not be suited more:
   To avenge my God and country in a single
          blow.
   Ah! Not for any far-flung friend,
    but by myself and for myself I'll tear
   this plague to tatters. For, who knows,
   tomorrow this selfsame murderer may turn
   his bloody hands on me. The cause of Laius
   therefore is my own.
          So, rise up, Children,
   and be off. Take your prayer boughs too.
   One of you will muster here the Cadmus
          clan.
   I am resolute and shall not stop
    till with Apollo's help all-blessed we
          emerge,
   or else all-cursed.

>>

[OEDIPUS *goes into the palace
followed by* CREON]

PRIEST: Children, rise.
The King has pledged us all our pleas
    and we have heard Apollo's voice. O may
    he visit us salvation from his hands
    and deal a death to all disease!

[*The* PRIEST *disperses the suppliants, and
the* CHORUS *of Theban Elders enters*]

ODE OF ENTRY

[*This first ode opens with a hymn to Apollo, the
god of victory and healing. Its stately dactylic
measure, as the* CHORUS *moves towards the altar
of Zeus, is bright with hope yet weighted with
awe and uncertainty. Then, as the Elders survey
the sufferings of Thebes, the rhythm changes
into one of dismay and excitement, broken by
sad lines of trochees and iambs. In the final
strophe and antistrophe the Elders clinch their
prayer for help on a note of energy and deter-
mination.*]

Strophe I

What god-golden voice from the gold-studded shrine of
                       the Pytho
    Comes to our glorious Thebes?
My spirit is tremulous, racked with its eagerness. Help,
    Healer of Delos—Paean!
I'm fainting with fear of what fate you will fashion me
                         now,
    Or turn in the turning of time.
Speak to me, Oracle—child everlastingly sprung
    From Hope so goldenly. Come!

Antistrophe I

I call on you first—God's daughter, immortal Athena!
    Then on your sister, earth's guardian,
Artemis ringed round with praises and throned in our
                        square.

    Ah! And far-shooting Phoebus.
You three that are champions hot to deliver, appear!
    For if ever the fire of disaster
Reared on the city, you beat its affliction away.
    Then come! Make yourselves ready today.

Strophe II

    Sorrows in a legion,
    Sorrows none can cipher.
    No shaft of wit or weapon
    For a people stricken.
    Shriveled soil and shrinking
    Wombs in childbirth shrieking.
    Soul after soul like fire
    Beats, beats upward, soaring
    To the god of the setting sun.

Antistrophe II

    A decimated city
    Dying. And deadly the dead,
    All lying uncried for. But crying
    Matrons and mothers graying
    At every altar praying,
    Till the chiming sorrow of dirges
    Is splintered by shouts of the paean:
    Rescue! O golden daughter
    Of Zeus's with your smile.

Strophe III

    Muffle the wildfire Mars,
    Warring with copper-hot fever.

>>>

Whirl him back homeward and headlong.
Plunge him down from our shores
Into Amphitrite's foaming
Lap or the únquiet grave
Of hissing Thracian seas.
For, O, what night has spared us
He does at break of day.
Zeus you sovereign of thunder,
Shiver him with lightning.

Antistrophe III

Aureate champion Apollo
Let us sing the song of your arrows
Shot from the bow of the sun;
While Artemis blazing with torches
Courses the Lýcean mountains.
And you, O Theban Bacchus,
Wine blushed, xanthic crowned,
You smiling god of succor,
Come all torchlit flaring,
Come wheeling with your Maenads,
Fall on the god that is godless.

[OEDIPUS *has entered*]

FIRST EPISODE

OEDIPUS: You pray! Then listen: what you pray for
you can have—remission of these miseries
and help—
if you'll hear my plan, a plan to stop the
plague.
I speak of course as stranger to the story
and stranger to the crime,
Helpless, therefore, to track it very far
unles. you lend me clues.
But since I am your latest citizen
speaking among citizens, I dare proclaim

to all you Thebans here the following:
Does any man among you know who killed
    Laius son of Labdacus?
                    Such a one
I now command to tell me everything.

                [*He pauses for a reply*]

If self-incrimination keeps him silent,
  let him be assured he need fear nothing
                          worse
  than banishment.

                [*He pauses again*]

Then is any man aware the murder was
                      committed
  by another from another land?
Let him not be shy to say it;
  I shall heap rewards on him,
  and Thebes her blessings.

                [*No one stirs*]

What! Silent still? If anyone
  is out to shield a guilty friend—
  or is it guilty self?—he'd better listen
  to the penalties I plan. That man,
  whoever that man be, I, this country's
  reigning king, cut off from every fellow-
                        ship
  of speech and contact, sacrifice and sacra-
                        ment,
  even ritual touch of water, in this realm.
Thrust out from every home he'll be
  the very picture of that pestilence
  god's oracle at Pythia has just revealed
                      to me.
Yes, such an ally, nothing less,
  am I of both religion and the murdered
                      man.

As to the killer,
  slipping off in singleness—or be it many
                      men—

I now call down a life to fit a life
   dragged out in degradation.
And if I myself should prove myself
   to have him in my halls an intimate,
   then on myself I call down every curse
   I've just invoked.

                This every jot and tittle
   I enjoin on you: for my sake,
   for the god Apollo, for this land—
   so fruitless now and so cast off by heaven.
For even without a sanction so divine
   how could you find it in you to neglect
   a monarch's death and not pursue
   this ending to the best of men? Whose
                very scepter
   I hold in my hands as King; his marriage
                bed
   my bed of seed; our children even shared
   with share of her, had he been blessed
              with progeny—
   O blessed, not cursed! Such ties
   swear me to his side as if he were my
                father.
I shall not rest until I've tracked the hand
   that slew the son of Labdacus, the son
   of Polydorus, heir to Cadmus in the line
   of ancient Agenor.

               And those who disobey
I'll ask the gods to curse with fields
   that never sprout and wombs that never
                flower.
The present plague can burn them up and
                worse.
The rest of you, my loyal men of Thebes,
   who think with me—may Justice champion
   and the whole of heaven help.

CHORUS: Sire, your oath will make a perjurer of me
   if I do not tell the truth. I swear
   I am not the killer nor can I show you

‹‹

who the killer is. Apollo posed the question,
it's up to him to point the culprit out.

OEDIPUS: Certainly, but who can force the hand of
heaven?

CHORUS: Then, the next best thing, if I may say . . .

OEDIPUS: Next best, third best, say it—anything!

CHORUS: There lives a man who with a king's eyes sees
the secrets of a king: Tiresias, of Apollo.
He is our source, our chance of learning,
King.

OEDIPUS: I know. Don't think that I've been marking
time.
Twice I have sent for him at Creon's bidding.
I cannot understand what keeps him so.

CHORUS: Well, we can forget those other tall old tales.

OEDIPUS: What tales? I must hear them all.

CHORUS: How he met his death through traveling
vagabonds.

OEDIPUS: I've heard that too. We have no witnesses,
however.

CHORUS: And he'd be a brazen man indeed who could
rest
in peace after all your menaces.

OEDIPUS: Mere words will not stay one whom murder
never could.

CHORUS: And yet there's one who will. Look!
They're slowly leading in the holy prophet,
sole temple of incarnate truth on earth.

[*The old and blind prophet*
TIRESIAS *is led in by a boy*]

OEDIPUS: Come, great mystic, Tiresias—intuitive,
didactic master of the finite and the in-
finite!

Though you cannot see it you must surely
feel
    the overwhelming weight of all this city's
worries.
You are our last refuge, Pontiff, and our help.
Apollo—if you have not heard the news—
    has sent back to us, who sent to him, an
answer
    saying: "No deliverance from the plague
except you seek and find the Laius killers
and punish such with death or banishment."
Now, sir, do not begrudge the smallest hint
    your skill from birds or any other omen
can elicit.
Save yourself, the city, and save me.
Save us from this whole corruption of the
dead;
    we're in your hands.
What more rewarding duty for a valiant man
    than stir himself to help where help he
can?

TIRESIAS: O, what anguish to be wise where wisdom
is a loss!
I thought I knew this well. What made me
come?

OEDIPUS: What makes you come so full of gloom?

TIRESIAS: O, send me home. Take up your load and I'll
take mine.
Believe me, it is better so.

OEDIPUS: That's no loyal answer! Refuse to speak?
Is it even filial to your town or fair?

TIRESIAS: Ah! Fair speech! If yours were only so
I should not shy away.

OEDIPUS: By all the gods,
do not deny us what you know!
We ask you, all of us, on bended knees.

‹‹

TIRESIAS: All ignorant! And I refuse to link
my utterance with a downfall such as
yours.

OEDIPUS: What! You know and will not say?
You'd rather sacrifice us all and let the city
rot?

TIRESIAS: I'd rather keep you and me from pain.
Don't press me uselessly, my lips are sealed.

OEDIPUS: What, nothing? You miserable old man!
You'd fire a stone to fury. Still insist?
Your flinty heart set in hopeless stubborn-
ness?

TIRESIAS: My flinty heart! O, if you could only see
what lurks in yours you would not chide
me so.

OEDIPUS: Hear that? What man alive, I ask, could stand
such insults to our sovereignty and state?

TIRESIAS: It will out in time. What if I hold my tongue?

OEDIPUS: Out in time! Then why not say it now?

TIRESIAS: No, I've said my say.
So choose your rage and fume away.

[*He begins to move off*]

OEDIPUS: I shall; I choose. I vent it all on you.
You, you planned this thing; and I
suspect you of the very murder even—
all but the actual stroke;
and if you had your eyes
I'd say you played that chief part too.

[TIRESIAS *turns back*]

TIRESIAS: Would you so? Then I shall charge you to
abide
by the very curse you trumpeted just now:
From this day forth keep far
from every person here and me—
The rotting canker in the state is you.

OEDIPUS: Insolence! And dare you think you're safe?

TIRESIAS: Yes, safe—for truth has made me strong.

OEDIPUS: What truth? Hardly learnt from your profession!

TIRESIAS: Learnt from you: who force it out of me.

OEDIPUS: Then, what? Say it again. I must have it straight.

TIRESIAS: Was it not straight? You'd bait and draw me on?

OEDIPUS: It made no sense; so speak it out again.

TIRESIAS: I say, you murdered the man whose murderer you require.

OEDIPUS: What! A second time? Now you won't escape.

TIRESIAS: Shall I add to it and make you angrier still?

OEDIPUS: To your heart's content. Mouth away nonsensities!

TIRESIAS: I say that you and your most dearly loved are wrapped together in a hideous sin— blind to the horror of it.

OEDIPUS: Exulting in abuse? You think you can go on?

TIRESIAS: Yes, unscathed—if truth is strength.

OEDIPUS: It is indeed! But not for you —you purblind man, in ears and mind and vision.

TIRESIAS: Ha! You've chosen just the wretched charge that soon with mockery they'll charge at you.

OEDIPUS: You can't hurt me, you night-hatched thing! Me or any man who lives in light.

TIRESIAS: I'm not the one that fate casts for your fall. Apollo is enough. It's in his able hands.

OEDIPUS: [*Remembering that it was* CREON *who urged him to send for* TIRESIAS, *Apollo's priest*] Creon! Was it you or he that thought up that?

TIRESIAS: Hardly Creon; you are your own worst
enemy.

OEDIPUS: O wealth and sovereignty, and art surpassing
art!

O life so pinnacled on fame!
What envy have you garnered to yourself?
And for a kingship which a state put in my
hands,

all given, never asked.
           So this
is what he wants, Creon the loyal,
Creon so long my friend! Stealing up
to overthrow and snatch! Suborning sor-
cerers

like this vamper-up of plots,
this hawking conjurer, a genius born blind
with eyes for gain. Yes, you! Tell me when
you ever played the prophet straight? Or
why

when the she-dog Sphinx of riddles sang,
you never spoke a thing to break the spell?
And yet her riddle called for insight trained,
no traveler's guess; which you plainly
showed

you did not have—either from theology or
birds.
But I, the Oedipus who stumbled here
without a hint, could snuff her out
by human wit, not taking cues from birds.
And I'm the one you want to topple down
to give yourself a place by Creon's throne.
Ah! Do not be surprised if exorcism turns
and exorcises you and him.
For were you not as doting as you seem,
I'd lash you with the lessons of your fraud.

*[The leader steps forward, lifting up
his hand in a gesture of restraint]*

CHORUS: Forgive us, Oedipus—but this is anger.
He spoke in anger too. And both beside the
point.

What we want to know is how
best to carry out the god's designs.

TIRESIAS: Perhaps you are a king, but I reign too—
in speech. I'll have my equal say. I'm not
your servant. I serve Loxian Apollo. So
don't ever put me down as Creon's myr-
midon.

I'm blind, you say; you mock at that! I say
you see and still are blind—appallingly:
blind to your origins and to a union
in your house. Yes, ask yourself where are
you from?
You'd never guess what hate is dormant in
your home
or buried with your dear ones dead;
or how a mother's and a father's curse
will one day scourge you with its double
thongs
and whip you staggering from the land.
It shall be night where now you boast the
day.

Then where shall your yelp of horror ring?
Where round the world to find a corner
on Mount Cithaeron not filled with echoes
when at last you see—yes soon!—what port-
less port
this palace and this marriage was you made
scudding in before a lucky breeze?
What plethora of sorrows—ah! you do not
dream—
will pull you down and level off your pride
to make it match your children and the
creature
that you are.

Go on then, hurl abuse
at everything that I or Creon say!
No man alive shall see his life so ground
away.

OEDIPUS: [*He steps forward threateningly*]

Ye gods! Must I listen to this thing?
Look, it dawdles! Does not rush to its perdi-
tion!
Does not turn—fly home in panic from my
halls!

TIRESIAS: You called me here. I never would have
come.

OEDIPUS: And I never thought to listen to such ranted
rot.
I'd not have hurried you in summons to my
home.

TIRESIAS: A born fool, of course, to you am I,
and yet to parents you were born from,
wise.

OEDIPUS: Parents? Wait! Who were my parents after
all?

TIRESIAS: [*Stops and turns*]

This single day will furnish you a birthday
and a death.

OEDIPUS: Such vague speech still! So wrapped in riddles!

TIRESIAS: And you so good, of course, at solving them?

OEDIPUS: Go on! You challenge there my strongest
point.

TIRESIAS: O yes! Your lucky strain. Your road to royal
ruin.

OEDIPUS: A ruin that saved a city. That's good enough
for me.

TIRESIAS: I'll take my leave, then. . . . Your hand boy
—home.

>>

OEDIPUS: Good! Let him take you home.
You're nothing but a nuisance here, an obstacle.
Your riddance is a blessing.

TIRESIAS: [*Stops and turns face-about*]

You'll not be rid of me until I've spoken
what I came to say. You do not frighten me.
There's not a thing that you can do to hurt.
I tell you this: the man you've searched for
all along with threats and fanfares for the murder
of King Laius—that man, I say, is here.
He was a stranger in our midst, they thought;
but in a moment you shall see
him openly displayed a Theban born,
and shattered by the honor. Blind
instead of seeing; beggar instead of rich;
he'll grope through foreign places tapping out
his way with stick in hand. O yes, detected
in his very heart of home: his children's father
and their brother; son and husband of his mother;
bed-rival to his father and assassin.
Ponder this and go inside,
and when you think you've caught me at a lie,
then come and tell me I'm not fit to prophecy.

[TIRESIAS *lets his boy lead him out*]

SECOND CHORAL ODE

[*The Elders, spurred on by the proclamation of* OEDIPUS, *begin to imagine with righteous and in-*

<<<<<<<<<<<<<<<<<<<<<<<<<<<<<<<<<<<<<<<<<<<<<<<

dignant anticipation what shall be the fate of the
man whose sin has plunged Thebes in misery.
The meter is swift and resolute. Then they re-
member the words of TIRESIAS and catch their
breath as their minds stumble over the terrible
possibility that OEDIPUS himself is implicated
(Strophe and Antistrophe II).]

Strophe I

Show me the man the speaking stone from Delphi damned,
  Whose hands incarnadine
Achieved the master stroke of master murdering.
Faster than horses that beat on the wind he must fly;
The son of Zeus caparisoned in light and fire
Is on his heels. The pack of sure-foot Fates
  Will track him down.

Antistrophe I

A Voice that coruscates from high Parnassian snows
  Leaps down like light:
Apollo to the hunt will run the man to earth.
Through savage woods and stony caverns
A lone wounded bull he limps—lost and alone—
Dodging living echoes from the mantic earth
  That sting and gad around him.

Strophe II

  Terrible auguries terribly trouble me—
   The seer's divining.
I cannot assent. I cannot deny. Deserted by words,
I hover on hopes—all blind for today and blind for to-
          morrow.
A division between the House of Laius and Polybus' son
   Today or yesterday
  I never knew; nor know of a quarrel
  Or a reason or challenge to challenge

The fame of Oedipus,
Though I seek to avenge the curious death
Of the Labdacid king.

Antistrophe II

Zeus and Apollo are wise and discern
The conditions of man.
But O among men—where is there proof that a prophet
can know
More than me a man? And yet, wisdom can surpass
Wisdom in a man. But nevertheless I'll not be quick
To judge before the proof.
For once the winged and female Sphinx
Challenged him and found him sage
And a friend of the city.
So never in *my* mind at least shall he be
Guilty of crime.

SECOND EPISODE

[CREON *comes in, distraught*]

CREON: Good citizens, I hurry here
shocked into your presence by a monstrous
charge
laid on me by Oedipus the King.
If he thinks in all this turmoil of our times
that any word or act of mine
was ever done in malice, done to harm,
I'd rather end my life than live so wronged.
For this is not a trifling calumny but full
catastrophe:
to find myself called traitor;
traitor to my town,
to you, and to my friends.

CHORUS: We are convinced the taunt was made in
anger,
not coolly uttered by a mind at calm.

‹‹

CREON: It was uttered, then? Said that I
      have got the seer to tell a tale of lies?

CHORUS: It was said. We cannot fathom why.

CREON: But said with steady eyes, steady mind—
      this onslaught made against my name?

CHORUS: I do not know. What my master does I do
              not see.
But look! He's coming from the house him-
              self.

[OEDIPUS *enters*]

OEDIPUS: What! You again? You dare come back?
You have the face to put your foot inside my
              door?
You, the murderer so self-proved,
      the self-condemned filcher of my throne!
In heaven's name what cowardice or lunacy
      did you detect in me
to give you courage for it? Did you think
that I would never spot such treachery,
such slinking jobbery, or that when I did
I'd not be one to fight? What madman's
            game is this:
to go out hunting crowns unbacked by
         money and by friends,
when crowns are won
by many friends and well-crammed money-
            bags?

CREON: Listen to me; do not be unfair.
Let *me* speak too, and when you've heard
         me, judge.

OEDIPUS: You're too good at talking, and I'm too bad
        at hearing
you—found so poisonous and so dangerous.

CREON: We'll take that very point up first.

OEDIPUS: We'll leave that very point alone—
      that you're no villain, eh?

CREON: Well, if you think that misinformed and fixed
ideas
are valuable you have an unfair mind.

OEDIPUS: Well, if you think that you can down a
relative
and get away scot-free you have an unbal-
anced mind.

CREON: All right, then—tell me what I've done?
What's the crime I've wronged you with?

OEDIPUS: Did you or did you not urge me to send
for that reverend frothy-mouthing seer?

CREON: I did. And still I think that I did right.

OEDIPUS: And how long is it since Laius chanced . . .

CREON: Laius what? What is it you mean to say?

OEDIPUS: Disappeared—died—was mysteriously dispatched?

CREON: Old calendars long past would tell us that.

OEDIPUS: And was this prophet in his practice then?

CREON: He was, and just as wise, just as honored.

OEDIPUS: Did he at any time then speak of me?

CREON: No. At least never in my hearing.

OEDIPUS: And you did nothing to investigate his death?

CREON: Of course we did: a commission, which drew
a blank.

OEDIPUS: But the all-seeing seer did not step forward
and all-see?

CREON: That I cannot answer for and shall not ven-
ture an opinion.

OEDIPUS: You could answer very well—at least upon a
certain point.

CREON: What point is that? If I know I shall not say
I don't.

OEDIPUS: Just this: were you not hand in glove with
him

‹‹

he'd never have thought of pinning Laius'
death on me.

CREON: If he means this, then you know best. It's my
turn now.
Let me ask and you can do the answering.

OEDIPUS: Ask away, but don't expect to find a murderer.

CREON: Well then, are you married to my sister?

OEDIPUS: I am. Why should I deny it?

CREON: And reign equally with her over all the
realm?

OEDIPUS: Yes. I do my best to carry out her wishes.

CREON: And of this twosome do I make an equal
third?

OEDIPUS: Exactly! Which is why you make so false a
friend.

CREON: No. Try to reason it as I must reason it.
First ask yourself who would choose
uneasy dreams to don a crown, when all
the kingly sway can be enjoyed without?
I could not covet kingship for itself
when I can be a king by other means.
Who would, who knows what wisdom is?
My kingly perquisites now come from you
untrammeled,
but, once a king, all hedged in by con-
straint.
How could I suit myself with power and
sovereignty
as now, if sovereignty once grasped were
grasped in pain?
I am not yet so mad as not to know
when I am suited gracefully with gain:
Now smiled upon by all; saluted now;
now drawn aside by suitors to the King,
my ear their door to hope.
Why should I let

this go, this ease, and reach for cares?
A mind at peace does not engender wars.
Treason never was my bent, nor I
    a man who parleys with an anarchist.

Test me, go to Delphi, ask if I
    have brought back lies for prophecies.
And do not stop, but if you find
    me plotting with a fortuneteller
take me, kill me, full-indicted
    on a double not a single count:
    not yours alone but mine.

        O do not judge
    me on a mere report, unheard!
No justice brands the good and justifies the
        bad.
Drive friendship out, I say, and you drive out
    life itself, one's sweetest friend.
Time will teach you well. The honest man
        needs time.
The sinner but a single day to bare his crime.

CHORUS: He speaks well, sire. The circumspect should
        care.
Swift thinking never makes sure thought.

OEDIPUS: Swift thinking must step in to parry
    where swift treachery steps in to plot.
Must *I* keep mum until his perfect plans
    are more than match for mine?

CREON: Then what is it you want—my banishment?

OEDIPUS: Banishment? Ha no! My plans for you are—
        death.
That will teach you how much envy's worth.

CREON: So adamant! So unconvinced! A rabid man!

OEDIPUS: Rabid, yes, for rights.

CREON: Then, all but mine.

OEDIPUS: Treason-monger!

CREON: Purblind sot!

OEDIPUS: But reigning still.

CREON: Yes, reigning fool!

OEDIPUS: O Thebes, my own poor Thebes!

CREON: My city too.

CHORUS: O Princes, please!
Look, Jocasta hurries from the house—
a timely balm on both your smarts.
You must compose your quarrel.

[JOCASTA *hurries in*]

JOCASTA: You wretched men! Out on all this senseless
clatter!

Shame to wrangle over private wrongs
with Thebes our city in her agonies!
Get back home sir, you; and Creon you
into your house. Stop turning trifles into
tragedies.

CREON: Trifles, sister! Oedipus your husband
plans to do me devilish harm, with choice
of dooms:
exile from my father's land, or death.

OEDIPUS: Yes, my wife; a plot against my person
is what I've caught him at: all cunningly
conspired.

CREON: God blight me dead so I be guilty
in the smallest part of what you charge!

JOCASTA: For God's sake listen, Oedipus. He's made
an oath to God; for me and for us all.

Strophe I

CHORUS: Believe her, King, believe! Be willing to be
wise!

OEDIPUS: What! You'd have me yield?

CHORUS: He never told
                                        you lies
          Before. He's sworn. Be kind.

OEDIPUS: You know for
                                      what you plead?

CHORUS: We know.

OEDIPUS: Explain.

CHORUS: .   Do not impeach a friend
                                            or lead
          Him to disgrace—his oath annulled upon a
                                              word.

OEDIPUS: It's come to that? My banishment or death
                                          preferred
          To what you want for him?

Strophe II

CHORUS: No, by Helios, no!
          God of the primal sun! Call gladless Death
                                        upon me—
          Godless, friendless—if that be in my mind.
          The dying land undoes me; sorrow heaped
                                        on sadness;
          Now to see you and him—combine in mad-
                                            ness.

OEDIPUS: Go then, let him go, till I go
          Abundantly to die;
          Or, flung from here and fated;
          Yours not his the cry that breaks me:
          He a thing that's hated.

CREON: Yes, how you hate—even in your yielding!
          But passion spent compunction follows!
          Such men justly bear tempers they created.

OEDIPUS: Get you gone, then! Leave me!

          [CREON goes, and OEDIPUS continues to stand
              where he is—disappointed and shaken]

Antistrophe I

CHORUS: Madam, why delay to lead him out?

JOCASTA: I stay
To know.

CHORUS: Hot and hasty words, suspicion
and dismay . . .

JOCASTA: From both?

CHORUS: From both.

JOCASTA: What words?

CHORUS: O let alone
The agony! Enough, enough! O let it lie!

OEDIPUS: You own,
I hope, you mealy-minded men of leniency,
To what a pass appeasement's brought you—
blunting me?

Antistrophe II

CHORUS: Sire, I've said it more than once, how insensate
We'd be, what crass and total fools, to abdi-
cate
From you, who set this foundering ship, this
suffering realm,
Back on her course and now again can take
the helm.

JOCASTA: In God's name, Oedipus, inform me too
What in the world has worked you to this
rage?

OEDIPUS: Willingly, my wife—so more to me than these.
It's Creon; he has played me false.

JOCASTA: What's the charge? Tell me clearly—what's
the quarrel?

OEDIPUS: He makes me murderer of Laius.

JOCASTA: His own invention, or on evidence?

OEDIPUS: Ah! The fox—he sends along a mouthing seer
            and keeps his own lips lily pure.

JOCASTA: O then, altogether leave behind
               these cares and be persuaded and con-
                                                soled.

            There is no art of seer-ship known to man:
               I have my proof. Yes, short and certain
                                                proof.

            Once long ago there came to Laius
               from—let's not suppose Apollo personally
               but from his ministers: an oracle,
               which said that fate would make him meet
                                                his end
            through a son, a son of his and mine.

            Well, there was a murder, yes; but done
               by foreign highwaymen—they say—where
                                                three
            highways meet. And secondly, the son,
               he at three days old is left by Laius
               (by other hands of course) upon a track-
                                                less
            hillside, his ankles linked together.

            So there! Apollo fails to make the son
               his father's murderer, or father (Laius
               sick with dread) murdered by his son.
            All foreseen by fate and seers, of course,
               and all to be forgotten.
            If God will have prognostications made,
               why, let God himself prognosticate!

OEDIPUS: My queen, each word that strikes my ear
               has struck at peace—struck at my very soul.

JOCASTA: You start! What pale memory passes now?

OEDIPUS: Laius was killed—I thought I caught the
                                                words—
            where three highways meet?

JOCASTA: So they said,
            and that is how the story goes.

OEDIPUS: The spot?
Where did the mishap fall?

JOCASTA: A land called Phocis;
at a spot where the road from Delphi
meets the road from Daulia.

OEDIPUS: And the time?
How many years ago?

JOCASTA: A little before
you came to power here the news was made
public in the town.

OEDIPUS: O Zeus! What plaything
will you make of me?

JOCASTA: Why, Oedipus—
what nightmare thought has touched you
now?

OEDIPUS: Don't ask!
Not yet! . . . Laius, tell me, his age? His
build?

JOCASTA: Tall: the first soft bloom of silver in his hair;
in form, not far removed from yours.

OEDIPUS: O lost! Yes, surely lost! Self-damned, I think,
just now and self-deceived.

JOCASTA: Self-what, my king?
That look you give—it chills.

OEDIPUS: I am afraid;
afraid the eyeless seer has seen. But wait—
one thing more . . .

JOCASTA: Yes? It frightens me,
but ask. . . . I'll try to tell.

OEDIPUS: Did he set out
in simple state or with a bodyguard as
King?

JOCASTA: Five men in all, and one a herald.
A single chariot for the King.

OEDIPUS: It's all too clear.
My wife, where did you get these details from?

JOCASTA: A servant. The only man who got away.

OEDIPUS: Is he in this house by chance?

JOCASTA: No. For, the moment he was back and saw
you reigning in dead Laius' place, he
begged
me, pressed my hand, to send him to the
country
far from sight of Thebes, where he could
live
a shepherd's life. And so I sent him.
Though
a slave, I thought he'd more than earned
this thanks.

OEDIPUS: Could we have him here without delay?

JOCASTA: Certainly. But what should make you ask?

OEDIPUS: There may be things, my wife, that I have
said,
best left unsaid; which makes me want
him here.

JOCASTA: He shall be here. But tell me Oedipus,
may *I* not also know what scares you so?

OEDIPUS: You shall. For I have passed into territories
of fear,
such threatenings of fate,
I welcome you, my truest confidante.

My father was Corinthian, Polybus.
My mother Dorian, called Merope.
I was the city's foremost man until
a certain incident befell—a curious
incident, though hardly worth the ferment
that it put me in.
                    At dinner once
a drunkard in his cups bawled out,

"Aha! Sham father's son!" And all that day
I fretted, hardly able to contain my hurt.
But on the next I went straightway to ask
my mother and my father; who were
shocked
to hear that anyone should say such things.

I was relieved by their response; and yet,
the thing had hatched a scruple in my
mind—
so deep it made me steal away from home
to Delphi, to the oracle, and there
Apollo—never hinting what I came to
hear—
packs me home again with ears ringing
with some other things he blurted out;
horrible disgusting things:
How mating with my mother I must spawn
a progeny to make men shudder; then,
be my very father's murderer.

O I fled from there. I measured out
the stars to put all heaven in between
the land of Corinth and such a damnéd
destiny.
And as I went, I stumbled on the very spot
where this king you say has met his end.

I'll . . . I'll tell the truth to you my wife.
As I reached this triple parting of the ways,
a herald and a man like you described
in a colt-drawn chariot came.
The leading groom—the old man urging
him—
tried to force me off the road. The groom
jostled me and I, infuriated,
landed him a blow. Which when the old
man sees,
he waits till I'm abreast,
then from his chariot cracks a double-
pointed

goad full down upon my head.
He more than paid for it. For in a trice
   this hand of mine had felled him with a
          stick
   and rolled him from the chariot stunned.
I killed them all.

Ah! If Laius is this unknown man,
   there's no one in the world so doomed as I.
There's no one born so ever cursed of God:
   a man, yes, whom no citizen nor even alien
   can let into his house; and no one greet;
   a man to force from homes.
And who but I have done it all? Myself,
   to fix damnation on myself! To clasp
   a dead man's wife with filthy hands; these
          hands
   by which he fell.
               Not hell-born then?
Not rotten to the core? A wretch! Yes I
   who have to flee yet fled can not go home
   to see my own; or I will make my mother
   wife, my father dead. My father
   Polybus who reared and gave me life.

The sight of this would make men right to
          say
   some living evil shadows me—O God!
Most holy God! Don't let that day begin,
   I'd rather disappear from man than see
   myself so beggared, dyed so deep in sin.

CHORUS: King, you tell us frightening things! But wait
      until you've heard the witness speak. Have
          hope.

OEDIPUS: Yes—all my hope upon a herdsman now?
      And I must wait until he comes.

JOCASTA: But when he comes what is it you want to
          hear?

OEDIPUS: Ah! Just this: if his account is yours, I'm
          clear.

:❮❮

JOCASTA: What was my account? What did I say?

OEDIPUS: Why, several highwaymen in your account
he claimed cut down the King. If he will
keep

to *several*, I, as only *one*, am not
the killer, not the same. But if he says
it was a lone man journeying—ah, then!—
the verdict tilts too heavily to me.

JOCASTA: You must believe me: his account was that,
exactly that. He cannot cancel what he
said.

The whole town heard, not I alone.
And even if he tries to change a word,
he still can never make—O surely, King!—
the death of Laius tally with the oracle,
which said it had to happen through a son
of mine . . .
poor mite who never killed a thing
but himself was killed—O long before!
After this, I'll never change my look
from left to right to suit a prophecy.

OEDIPUS: I like your reasoning. And yet . . . and yet . . .
that herdsman . . . have him here. Do not
forget.

JOCASTA: Immediately. But let us go indoors.
All my care is you, and all my pleasure yours.

[OEDIPUS *and* JOCASTA *go into the palace*]

THIRD CHORAL ODE

[*The Elders seem at first merely to be expressing
a lyrical admiration of purity of heart and piety,
but before the end of the ode we see that the
reputation itself of* OEDIPUS *is at stake.* JOCASTA's
apparent impiety has shocked the CHORUS *into
realizing that if divine prophecies cannot go un-
fulfilled and man's insolence unpunished, then*

OEDIPUS *himself, whoever he is, must be weighed in the balance. It is too late to go back; a choice will have to be made. They call desperately on Zeus.*]

Strophe I

O purity of deed and sweet intent!
Enshrine me in your grace
A minister to radiant laws
Heaven born which have
No father but Olympus nor
Fading genesis from man.
Great is God in them
And never old
Whom no oblivion lulls.

Antistrophe I

Pride engenders power, pride:
Banqueting on vanities
Mistaken and mistimed;
Scaling pinnacles to dash
Her foot against Fate's stone.
But patriotic piety
May God protect—
My God my constant champion.

Strophe II

Let a brazen man parade
Impiety and brash disdain
Of principalities and canons.
Then dog him Doom and pay him Pride
Wages for his wanton sins
(Until his gain be gain of good)
Of sacrilege and folly.
What shield is there for such a man
Against God's righteous arrows?

Could I celebrate such wickedness
And celebrate the dance?

Antistrophe II

I shall not worship at the vent
Where oracles from earth are breathed,
Nor at Abae's shrine and not
Olympia, unless these oracles
Are justified—writ large—to man.
Zeus, if king of kings you are,
Then let this trespass not go hidden
From you and your great eye undying.
Your Laius prophecies are turned to lies;
They fade away with reverence gone
And honor to Apollo.

THIRD EPISODE

[JOCASTA *hurries in from the palace with a garlanded
olive branch in her hand and a burning censer*]

JOCASTA: Men of State, I have a new design:
                 with these garlands and with incense in
                                           my hands
                   to call at all the shrines.
             For rampant fancies in a legion raid the mind
                 of Oedipus; he is so far from sense
                   he cannot gauge the present from the past
                   but pins his soul to every word of fear.
             All my advice is bankrupt; I address
                 myself to you Apollo whose Lycean shrine
                   is nearest to these rites and prayers,
                   that you may work some way to make us
                                           clean.
             For we are gone to pieces at the sight
                 of him the steersman of the ship astray by
                   fright.

[*While* JOCASTA *is kneeling in prayer
a* MESSENGER *from Corinth enters*]

MESSENGER: Can you tell me please, good sirs,
where is the palace of King Oedipus or best
the King himself, if he is anywhere?

CHORUS: This is his palace, sir, and he's within;
this lady is his wife and mother . . . of his
children.

MESSENGER: Heaven bless her always and bless hers—
the perfect wife blessed perfectly with
him!

JOCASTA: And you sir, too, be blessed for your remark. . . .
But are you here to ask us news or give?

MESSENGER: To give it, madam: happy news both for
your house and husband.

JOCASTA: Happy news! From where?

MESSENGER: From Corinth. O a pleasing piece of news!
Or I'd think so . . . Perhaps a little bittersweet.

JOCASTA: What's bittersweet? What's half-and-half to
please?

MESSENGER: King Elect of Isthmia is he.
Ready—so they hope—to mount the throne.

JOCASTA: How's that? The old man Polybus still reigns.

MESSENGER: No more. For death has sealed him in his
grave.

JOCASTA: What? Is Oedipus's father dead?

MESSENGER: Yes, dead. It's true. On my life he's dead.

[JOCASTA *excitedly turns to maidservant*]

JOCASTA: Quick, girl—off and tell your master this!
Aha! Forecasts of the gods where are you
now?
This is the man that Oedipus
was in a fright to kill; so fled, and now

ᒻᒻᒻᒻᒻᒻᒻᒻᒻᒻᒻᒻᒻᒻᒻᒻᒻᒻᒻᒻᒻᒻᒻᒻᒻᒻᒻᒻᒻᒻᒻ

OEDIPUS: without the smallest push from him—he's
                                          dead.

[*Enter* OEDIPUS]

OEDIPUS: Jocasta, dearest wife,
      why have you called me from the palace
                                 here?

JOCASTA: Just listen to this man and fill your ears:
      how dwindled are the grand predictions
                               of Apollo!

OEDIPUS: Who is this? What has he come to say?

JOCASTA: A man from Corinth, come to let you know
      your father is no more. Old Polybus is
                                   dead.

OEDIPUS: What's that? Explain yourself, good sir.

MESSENGER: Why, to give you first news first, he's gone.
      Be quite assured—he's dead.

OEDIPUS: By treason or
                                       disease?

MESSENGER: A little touch will tip the old to sleep.

OEDIPUS: He died a natural death, then? Poor old man!

MESSENGER: A natural death, by right of many years.

OEDIPUS: Ah! Undone then! . . . Well, my wife, and
                                   I am done
      with delving into Pythian oracles—
      this jangled mongering with birds on high,
      which foretold—yes, had it all arranged—
      that I should kill my father. Ha! He's dead
      and under sods, whilst here I stand,
      my sword still in its scabbard. . . . Or did
                                   he pine for me?
      And did I kill him so? . . . Well, he's dead!
      And may he rest in peace with all those
                                   prophecies
      (worth nothing now) in Hades Halls.

JOCASTA: Worth nothing—as I told you even then!

OEDIPUS:	You told me, yes; but I was sick with fear.
JOCASTA:	Forget it all. Give none of it a thought.
OEDIPUS:	There is that scruple of my mother's bed.
JOCASTA:	How can a man have scruples when it's only Chance that's king?
	There's nothing certain, nothing preordained;
	it's best to live by chance as best we may.
	Forget this silly thought of mother-marrying.
	Why, many men in dreams have married mothers,
	and he lives happiest who makes the least of it.
OEDIPUS:	Everything you say would make good sense were my mother not alive—she is;
	so all your comfort cannot quiet me.
JOCASTA:	At least your father's grave has lightened up the scene.
OEDIPUS:	It has, but now I fear a woman's life.
MESSENGER:	A woman's, sir? Who ever could she be?
OEDIPUS:	Merope, old man, who lives with Polybus.
MESSENGER:	But what's in her that she can frighten you?
OEDIPUS:	There's been a warning—warning sent from heaven.
MESSENGER:	Can it be told—or is it not to be divulged?
OEDIPUS:	No, you may be told: Apollo once declared that *I* would come to couple with my mother,
	and with these hands of mine spill out the life-blood of my father. All of which has put me far and long from Corinth; in sweet prosperity maybe, but what's so sweet
	as looking into parents' eyes?
MESSENGER:	Is this the fear that drove you out of Corinth?

ᚼᚼᚼᚼᚼᚼᚼᚼᚼᚼᚼᚼᚼᚼᚼᚼᚼᚼᚼᚼᚼᚼᚼᚼᚼᚼᚼᚼᚼᚼᚼᚼᚼᚼᚼᚼᚼ

OEDIPUS: This, old man, and not to kill my father.

MESSENGER: Then why do I wait? I've come to save.
I can unlock the worries of a king.

OEDIPUS: Ah! If you could, I'd heap you with rewards.

MESSENGER: Ah! That's why I came; to bring you home
and do myself some good.

OEDIPUS: No, not home,
I'll not go near a parent still.

MESSENGER: My son,
it's plain you don't know what you're at.

OEDIPUS: Speak out, old man. For God's sake, tell
me—what?

MESSENGER: Well, you've fled from home because of this?

OEDIPUS: Yes; and fear Apollo may prove right.

MESSENGER: And you be fouled by what your parents are?

OEDIPUS: Yes, old man, it's that. I'm always haunted
by that dread.

MESSENGER: Then, don't you understand: you're terrified
for nothing?

OEDIPUS: Nothing? How—when I am their son?

MESSENGER: Because Polybus and you were worlds apart.

OEDIPUS: Worlds apart? He was my father, wasn't he?

MESSENGER: No more nor less than I who tell you this.

OEDIPUS: No more nor less than you? Than nothing
then.

MESSENGER: Exactly so. He never gave you life, no more
than I.

OEDIPUS: Then, whatever made him call me son?

MESSENGER: You were a gift. He took you from my arms.

OEDIPUS: What! He loved enough to take another's
child?

MESSENGER: Yes—he had no children of his own to love.

OEDIPUS: But was I born or bought, this gift you gave?

MESSENGER: Discovered in a woody dell of Cithaeron.

[JOCASTA *moves away from the others—she
has suddenly gone pale*]

OEDIPUS: On Theban hills? What made you wander
here?

MESSENGER: On these hills I used to tend my flocks.

OEDIPUS: What! A shepherd out for hire?

MESSENGER: And on that day your savior, too, my son.

OEDIPUS: But did you find me in great misery or pain?

MESSENGER: The ankles of your feet could tell you that.

OEDIPUS: Ah! That ancient hurt! Why remind me of it?

MESSENGER: I loosed your feet, both riveted together.

OEDIPUS: My birthmark and my brand from babyhood!

MESSENGER: Which gave you also your unlucky name.

OEDIPUS: My mother's doing or my father's?
For God's sake, say.

[JOCASTA *hides her face in her hands*]

MESSENGER: I do not know.
The man who gave you me could tell.

OEDIPUS: What, received at secondhand? Not found
by you?

MESSENGER: Not found by me, but handed over by another shepherd.

OEDIPUS: What shepherd? Could you point him out?

MESSENGER: I think he went by name as one of Laius'
men.

OEDIPUS: You mean the king's who reigned here long
ago?

MESSENGER: Exactly so. It was a herdsman of that king.

OEDIPUS: Could I see him? Is he still alive?

MESSENGER: Your own compatriots could tell you best.

OEDIPUS: [*Turns toward the* CHORUS]

Does any man here present know
    this herdsman he is talking of—
    either seen him in the fields or here?
Speak. The time has come for full discovery.

CHORUS: I think he means that herdsman, sir,
    you asked to see before. Jocasta here
    is surest judge of that.

                [*They all turn toward* JOCASTA,
                    who stands transfixed]

OEDIPUS: Come, madam, do you know the man we sent
                    for once before?
Is he the one he means?

JOCASTA: [*Wildly*]

Who? What matters who he means? Why
                    ask?
Forget it all. It's not worth knowing now.

OEDIPUS: Forget it all? I can't stop now.
Not with all my birth clues in my hands!

JOCASTA: For God's sake don't proceed. For your own
                    life's sake.
And *I've* been tortured long enough.

OEDIPUS: O come! It won't be you that is disgraced
    even if I'm proved a thrice-descended
                    slave.

                [JOCASTA *throws herself before him
                    and clutches his knees*]

JOCASTA: Yet, be persuaded, please. Do *not* proceed.
OEDIPUS: Persuaded from the truth? Pursuing it?
No. I *must* proceed.

JOCASTA: Though I'm pleading
    for your happiness!

OEDIPUS: That happiness
    has plagued me long enough.

                [JOCASTA *slowly rises*]

JOCASTA: God help you, Oedipus!
God hide it from you: who you are!

OEDIPUS: Will someone go and fetch the herdsman
here?
We'll leave the lady to her high descent.

JOCASTA: Good-bye, my poor deluded, lost and
damned!
There's nothing else that I can call you now.

[*She rushes out*]

CHORUS: Oedipus, what made the Queen so wildly
leave—
struck dumb? A silence just before a storm!

OEDIPUS: Storm, then, burst away! Though I be proved
born from nothing let me find that nothing
out.
And let the Queen with all her woman's
pride
bridle at my paltry origin.
O I'm a child of Chance, a lucky child!
I shall not blush to own her motherhood.
Her moons my monthly cousins watched me
wax and wane.
My fealty to that family makes me move
true to myself. My family I shall prove.

FOURTH CHORAL ODE

[*The Elders, forgetting for the time being* JO-
CASTA's *ominous withdrawal, anticipate the joy
of discovering who Oedipus really is. Ironically,
they already think of themselves as celebrating
the good that will come of it.*]

Strophe I

If *I* am a prophet with sapient eyes
Sweet Cithaeron you in the moon of tomorrow

Shall not—by Olympus!—lack
Shouts of your name as the nurse and the mother,
Compatriot—yes!—of Oedipus.
We shall weave you with dances
For your pleasing our princes.
May it please you Apollo,
Hail great Healer!

Antistrophe I

Who was your mother, child? Which of the dryads,
Perennially young, did Pan of the mountains have?
Or was it Apollo haunting high
Savannas? Or Mercury king of Cyllene's
Summits? Or were you presented to Bacchus by
(He of the pinnacles) some Heliconian
Nymph—amongst whom
He frequently frolics?

FOURTH EPISODE

OEDIPUS: [*Gazing at a figure, old and rough-
clad, who now approaches*]

Look, Elders!
If I may play the prophet too, I'd say—
    although I've never met the man—
        there's the herdsman we've been searching
            for:
    he's old enough and matches this old man.
But you no doubt can better judge than I,
    you've seen the man before.

CHORUS: We know him well.
Laius never had a better servant.

[*The* SHEPHERD *enters, obviously ill at ease.* OEDIPUS
surveys him and turns to the MESSENGER]

OEDIPUS: First question then to you, Corinthian:
    is he the man you mean?

MESSENGER: The very man.

OEDIPUS: Come here, sir, and look me in the eyes.
Tell me straight—were you ever Laius's?

SHEPHERD: Yes sir, born and bred, sir—never bought.

OEDIPUS: You were employed as . . . how did you
spend your days?

SHEPHERD: Chiefly as a shepherd, sir.

OEDIPUS: A shepherd where?
What was your terrain?

SHEPHERD: Cithaeron—
or mainly places near.

OEDIPUS: Good, then
you've run across this man before?

[*The* SHEPHERD *tries to avoid
looking at the* MESSENGER]

SHEPHERD: How'd
he be there, sir?
Who do you mean, sir?

OEDIPUS: The man in front of you.
Did you ever meet him?

SHEPHERD: Not to remember,
sir. . . .
I couldn't rightly say.

MESSENGER: And no wonder, sire!
But let me jog his memory. I'm sure
he won't forget the slopes of Cithaeron
where for three half-years we were neigh-
bors
he and I—he with two herds, I with one—
from spring to early autumn, six long
months.
And when at last the winter came we both
drove off our flocks: I to my sheepcotes,
he back to Laius' folds. . . .
Am I right or am I wrong?

◄◄◄

SHEPHERD: [*Sullenly*]
Aye, you're right,
but it was long ago.

MESSENGER: Now tell me this:
do you recall a certain baby boy
you gave me once to bring up as my own?

SHEPHERD: What're you getting at? What're these questions for?

MESSENGER: Take a look, my friend: he's standing there,
your baby boy!

SHEPHERD: Damn you man! Can you not be still?

OEDIPUS: Watch your words, sir!
It's you who ought to be rebuked, not he.

SHEPHERD: Great master, please!
Tell me where I'm wrong.

OEDIPUS: You refuse to answer
this man's questions on the baby boy.

SHEPHERD: But, sir, this man's inventing—
why he doesn't know a thing!

OEDIPUS: You won't
talk for pleasure?
Then, perhaps you'll talk for pain.

[*Raises his hand to strike*]

SHEPHERD: For God's sake, sir, don't hurt a poor old man.

OEDIPUS: Here, someone, twist the wretch's hands behind his back.

SHEPHERD: God help me, sir! What is it you must know?

OEDIPUS: That baby he's been speaking of—did you
give it him or not?

SHEPHERD: I did, I did! I wish I'd died that day.

OEDIPUS: You'll die today
unless you speak the truth.

SHEPHERD: Much sooner, sir,
if I speak the truth.

OEDIPUS: This man, it's clear, is playing for time.

SHEPHERD: No, not me, sir! I've said already I gave it him.

OEDIPUS: Then, where's it from? Your home or someone else's?

SHEPHERD: O not mine, sir! I got it from another.

OEDIPUS: Someone here in Thebes? Of what house?

SHEPHERD: For the love of God, sir, please don't ask me any more!

OEDIPUS: If I have to ask again—you're dead.

SHEPHERD: Then . . . from Laius's house—that's where it's from.

OEDIPUS: What! A slave? Or someone of his line?

SHEPHERD: O God! Must I bring myself to say it?

OEDIPUS: And I to hear. Yes, it must be heard.

SHEPHERD: They say it was . . . actually his own. But the Queen inside could probably explain.

OEDIPUS: She, *she* gave it you?

SHEPHERD: Just that, my Lord.

OEDIPUS: With what intention?

SHEPHERD: To do away with it.

OEDIPUS: The child's own mother?

SHEPHERD: There'd been a holy warning.

OEDIPUS: What kind of warning?

SHEPHERD: That he would be a parent-killer.

OEDIPUS: In heaven's name what made you pass him on to this old man?

SHEPHERD: Only pity, sir. I thought he'd take him home and far away. Never this—O never kept for infamy!

>>

          For if you are the one he says you are,
                make no mistake: you are a doom-born
                                              man.

                          [OEDIPUS *stares in front of him,*
                                    then staggers forward]

OEDIPUS: Lost! Ah lost! At last it's blazing clear.
            Light of my eyes, good-bye—my final gaze!
            My birth all sprung revealed from those it
                                      never should;
                myself entwined with those I never could;
                and I the killer of those I never would.

                          [OEDIPUS *rushes into the palace*]

FIFTH CHORAL ODE

[*The Elders, seeing that the case of* OEDIPUS *is
lost, break into a solemn and a passionate lament
for the insecurity of all human fame—so bitterly
exemplified now in the fall of the once confident*
OEDIPUS.]

Strophe I

O the generations of man!
His life is vanity and nothingness.
Is there one, one,
Who more than tastes of, thinks of, happiness,
Which in the thinking vanishes?
Yours the text, yours the spell,
I see it in you Oedipus:
Man's pattern of unblessedness.

Antistrophe I

You who aimed so high!
Who hit life's topmost prize—success!
Who—Zeus, O who—

Struck and toppled down the griffin-taloned
Deathknell witch, and like our saving tower
Soared above the rotting shambles here:
A sovereign won, supremely blest,
A king of mighty Thebes.

Strophe II

And now what tale, what turn of fate,
And what such friend, was ever found of sorrow?
The majesty, the fame,
Of Oedipus cut down and father son
Found sharing ample anchorage.
O father's field all double-tilled!
How did you, could you, fructify so long
And not break out in horror?

Antistrophe II

Caught in the end by Time
Who always sees, where Justice sits as judge,
Your unwed wedding's done,
Begetter and begot—O Son of Laius!
Out of sight what sight might not have seen!
My sorrow heaves, my lips lament,
Which drew their breath from you and now
Must quiver in repose.

EPILOGUE

[*A palace* OFFICIAL *hurries out from the palace*]

OFFICIAL: Listen, Lords most honorable of Thebes:
forget the House of Labdacus, all filial
sympathy,
if you would stop your ears, hide your eyes,
not break your hearts against appalling
pain.
Even Ister even Phasis with their waters
could not flush away, I think, the sin

CHORUS: Stop. There is no jot or tittle lacking
   from the agony that loads us now.

OFFICIAL: I'll tell it quick and you can quickly hear:
   Jocasta's gone, the Queen.

CHORUS: Unhappy lady! How?

OFFICIAL: Self-destroyed! The pain of it
   you shall be spared who were not there,
     and I
   from my poor memory shall recount the
     struggles
   of that lost princess.

       The moment she had
     burst
   into the house—running through the doors
     demented—
   she made for the bridal bed, plunging her
     fingers
   through her hair; and slamming shut the
     doors behind her
   sobbed out Laius' name (so long dead),
   recalling the night his love had bred his
     murderer
   and left a mother making cursed
   children with her son.
        "Unhappy bed!"
   she wailed, "twice wicked soil! The father's
   seedbed nurtured for the mother's son!"
And then she killed herself. I don't know how.
The final act escaped our eyes—
   all fastened now upon the raving Oedipus
   who broke upon us, stamping up and down
   and shouting out: "A weapon, quick!
Where is the brideless bride?
Find me that double breeding ground

where, sown the mother, now has sown the
son."

Some instinct of a demigod discovered her to
him,
not us near by. As if led on,
he smashes hollering through the double
doors
breaking all its bolts and lunges in.
And there we saw her hanging, twisted, tangled,
from a halter—sight that wrings from him
a maddened cry. He frees the noose and
lays
the wretched woman down, then—O
hideous sequel!—rips from off her dress
the golden brooches she was wearing,
holds
them up, and rams them home right
through his eyes.
"Wicked, wicked eyes!" he gasps,
"You shall not see me nor my shame—
not see my present crime.
Go dark, for all time blind
to what you never should have seen, and
blind
to those this heart has cried to see."

And as this dirge went up so did his hands
to strike his founts of sight, not once but
many times.
And all the while his eyeballs gushed
in bloody dew upon his beard . . . no, not
dew,
no oozing drops—a spurt
of black-ensanguined rain like hail beat
down.

A coupled punishment upon a coupled sin:
husband and wife one flesh in their disaster;

their happiness of long ago—true happiness—
now turned to tears this day; to ruin, death
and shame;
no evil absent by whatever cursed name.

CHORUS: Unhappy man! And is he still in pain?

OFFICIAL: He shouts for the barriers to be unbarred and
he
displayed to all of Thebes—his father's
murderer,
his mother's—no, a word too foul to say—
as if he means to cast himself adrift,
not rot at home the curser and the cursed.

His strength is gone he needs a helping hand;
his wound and weakness more than he can
bear.

But you will see. The doors are opening,
look:
such a sight that turns all loathing into
tears.

[OEDIPUS, *the blood still streaming
from his eyes, stumbles in*]

CHORAL DIALOGUE

CHORUS: O, O, most inhuman vision!
A world of pain outsuffered and outdone.
You poor possessed! By what possessed?
What devil pounced on you with devil's
doom?
I cannot look—and yet, so much to ask,
So much to know, so much to see—
I cannot look for shuddering.

OEDIPUS: I am deserted, dark,
Yes, where is sorrow stumbling?
Whence flits that voice so near?
Where, Spirit, have you driven me?

CHORUS: To a doom no voice can speak nor eye regard.

Strophe I

OEDIPUS: Ah! A nightmare mist has fallen
Adamantine black for me—
Abomination closing.
Cry, cry, O cry again!
Those needle pains
Are pointed echoes of my sinning.

CHORUS: Such great sufferings are not strange
Where double pains must make a double
sorrow.

Antistrophe I

OEDIPUS: O you my friend,
Still friend and by my side!
Still staying by the blindman!
Your form eludes, your voice is clear;
That voice lights up my darkness.

CHORUS: Man of havoc, how
Could you hate your sight so?
What demon so possessed you?

Strophe II

OEDIPUS: Friends, it was Apollo,
Spirit of Apollo:
He made this fruit of evil fructify.
O yes, I pierced my eyes—
My useless eyes—why not?
When all that's sweet
Had parted from my vision.

CHORUS: These things are so; are as you say.

OEDIPUS: Nothing left to see, to love,
Nothing to enjoy,
No welcome in communion.
Friends, who are my friends,

Hurry me from here,
Hurry off the monster:
That deepest damned
And god-detested man.

CHORUS: A man both lost in make and mind,
We wish that we had never known you.

Antistrophe II

OEDIPUS: Yes, rot that man's unlocking
My feet from biting fetters!
Preserving me from murder to no profit.
Had I only died then
I should not now be leaving
All I love and mine
So sadly shattered.

CHORUS: Your wish is also ours.

OEDIPUS: Yes, I should be free,
Free from parricide;
Not pointed out as wedded
To the one who weaned me.
Now I'm god-abandoned
A son of sin and sorrows,
All incest-sealed with the womb that bore
me.

O Oedipus, your portion!

CHORUS: How can we say that your design was good?
To live in blindness? Better live no longer.

OEDIPUS: Enough of this! Enough of your advice!
It was a good design. Don't tell me otherwise.

My best design! What kind of eyes should I
need

to gaze upon my father's face
in Hades Halls, or my unhappy mother's?
Or eyes that could be eyes that saw
my children's faces? Joy? No, no—a sight
of pain

engendered from these loins.

Or eyes to see
citadel and tower and holy idoled shrine
I cast away?—most cursed I
the Prince of princes here in Thebes
and now self-damned and self-appointed
pariah,
the refuse-heap of heaven on display as son
of Laius;
parading and self-dyed in sin. . . .
What! Eyes to lift and gaze at these?
O no, none, none! Rather plug my ears
and choke that stream of sound,
stuff the senses of my carcass dumb—
glad to stifle voices with my vision;
sweet to lift away the soul from hurt!

Pity you, Cithaeron, that you gave me har-
bor,
took me in and did not kill me straight;
that you did not hush my birth from man.

Pity you, Polybus, and Corinth,
age-old home I called my father's.
What fair skin you housed around what foul-
ness!
A prince of sin revealed and son of sinners.

And you three roads and dell concealed,
you copse of oak and straitened triple
ways!
I handed you my blood to drink—the chalice
of my father's. O what memories have you
of my manners then, or what I did
when after that I came here?

Yes, you batch of weddings! Birthdays breeding
seedlings from their very seed.
Fathers, sons and brothers flourishing in foul-
ness
with brides and wives and mothers in a

‹‹‹

                    monstrous coupling;
    unfit to tell what's too unfit to touch.

    By all the gods, then, hide me somewhere far
        and soon, or kill me, drown me in the seas,
        away forever from your vision. Come!
    Take the broken man. Don't shrink from
                    touch.
    My load is mine, don't fear. No man could
               bear so much.

CHORUS: Wait! Here Creon comes to hear your woes
        and deal with your designs. He takes your
                   place
    as sole custodian of the State.

OEDIPUS: Ah! What words are left for me to him?
    What title to sincerity and trust
        when all my past behavior's proved so
                  wrong?

                    [*Enter* CREON]

CREON: It's not to scoff or scorn for past behavior,
        Oedipus, that I have come . . . [*Turns to*
                    attendants]
    You there, show some reverence for the dig-
        nity of man,
    and blush at least before Apollo's royal sun,
    which feeds the world with fire,
    to so display unveiled putrescence
    in its very picture of decay
    assaulting earth, the heaven's rain, the
              light of day.
    Quickly take him home. A family's ears, a
             family's eyes,
    alone should know a family's miseries.

OEDIPUS: For God's own love, you best of men
        who visit me the worst
        with clemency beyond my dreams
        grant me one request—I ask it
        for your sake not mine.

CREON: What favor could
           you want of me?

OEDIPUS: Expel me quickly, purge
           me far from Thebes, to where no human
                                voice is heard.

CREON: This I would have done—ah!—long ago
           had not first I wished to know God's will.

OEDIPUS: God's will is open, all his oracle is clear:
           kill the impious one, the parricide, kill me.

CREON: So ran the words, but in these straits
           it's best to ask the god what should be
                                done.

OEDIPUS: What! Interrogations for a thing so down?

CREON: Yes, for even you would now believe the god.

OEDIPUS: Then add to it this charge, I beg, this prayer:
           her poor remains still in the house,
           bury them—what tomb you wish; you will
           not fail your own with proper rites.

           But as for me, my father's city here
           must never harbor me alive. So let
           me live among the hills, yes, Cithaeron,
           called my mountain which my mother
           and my father gave me while they lived
           to be my tomb. And there I'll be obedient
           to the death they planned.
                                And yet I know
           no sickness and no natural death
           will sever me from life—no, not me, pre-
                                served
           from death precisely for disaster. . . . So
           let my fortune follow where it lists. . . .

           Now for my children, first of all my sons:
           these you need not care for, Creon.
           They are men; they'll always find a liveli-
                                hood.
           But my girls, that little pair of orphans
           both so sad, whose place at table

‹‹‹

never missed being set with mine; who
ate with me;
shared everything I had—ah! these
look after for me, guard them both.

[CREON *goes to fetch* OEDIPUS's *two little daughters,
Antigone and Ismene. Meanwhile,* OEDIPUS, *thinking
he is still there, continues to plead*]

If only I could touch them with my hands
and weep my fill! Good Creon—one last
time!

Just touch them . . . please, you generous
king! So let
me fancy them within my arms as when I
saw.

[CREON *returns leading Antigone
and Ismene by the hand*]

But wait! That sound? Those children's
voices?
Ah, don't tell me—my two darlings crying!
Has Creon pitied me and sent me all my
heart's desire?
Could that be true?

CREON: It is.
I ordered it, to stir again your old delight.

OEDIPUS: God bless you, Creon, bless your path
through life;
encompass you with surer joys than mine.
But children, where, where are you? Hurry,
come
into these . . . these brother's arms . . .
these arms of mine,
which have struck out the light
and made your father's face this eyeless
mask.
Ah! Children, he was blind and blank and
now
revealed your father in full view—
the sower and the seed.

No power to view you now but only weep,
 and ponder on that bitter time to come
 which cruel consort with the world will
            prove.
No days of state, no gay attendances
 from which you will not hurry home in
             tears:
 tears for holidays.

       And then one day
 a marriage time will come—and who will
            marry you?
Who in this world will face the destiny
 that dogs our line? Its sex-linked heritage!
Our record too replete! Your father killed
 his father, tilled the womb again from
           which he sprang,
 to raise a generation—you—
 from his bed of birth. Yes, they'll point at
             you.
Who will want to marry you?
O there's none—my little ones, not one!
And life for you is all decline: a doom
 to empty spinsterhood.

        [*Turns to* CREON]
Listen, Son of Menoeceus:
 now their natural parents are no more
 they have no other father left but you.
You must not see your blood go down in
           beggary
 or watch them roaming husbandless;
 you must not leave them to a fate like
             mine.
Open your heart. Look, they're young! Bereft
 of everything unless you furnish it.
Come—a promise, noble prince, your hand!
      [CREON *gives his hand*]
Now, darling children, if you could under-
            stand

<<<<<<<<<<<<<<<<<<<<<<<<<<<<<<<<<<<<<<<<<

        I'd tell you, O, so many things!
        Let this suffice, a simple prayer:
            abide in modesty so may you live
            the happy life your father did not have.

CREON: These tears . . . enough! Now go inside.

OEDIPUS: I must, with bitterness.

CREON: There is a time
        for all good things.

OEDIPUS: You know my terms?

CREON: I'll know them when you tell me them.

OEDIPUS: Then banish me.

CREON: You ask what's God's to give.

OEDIPUS: God's enemy?

CREON: A swifter answer then!

OEDIPUS: Ah! Do you mean it?

CREON: What I do not mean, I do not say.

OEDIPUS: Then, lead me off.

CREON: Come! Let go your children. Come!

OEDIPUS: No, no, never! Don't take them from me.

CREON: Stop being master now—
        the mastery you had in life has meant so
            little.

       [OEDIPUS *is led away into the palace.*
          The doors are closed]

CHORUS: Citizens of our ancestral Thebes,
        look on this Oedipus, the mighty and once
            masterful,
        elucidator of the riddle,
        envied on his pedestal of fame.
       You saw him fall; you saw him swept away.
       So, being mortal, look on that last day
         and count a man not blessed in his life
            until
        he's crossed life's bounds unstruck by ruin
            still.

Oedipus at Colonus

for MARTIN W. TANNER

"he setteth his mind to finish
his work, and watcheth to
polish it perfectly."

THE CHARACTERS

OEDIPUS: ex-king of Thebes

ANTIGONE: his daughter

A COUNTRYMAN

CHORUS of old men of Colonus

ISMENE: sister of Antigone

THESEUS: king of Athens

CREON: present king of Thebes

POLYNEICES: son of Oedipus

MESSENGER

Soldiers and attendants

TIME AND SETTING

Some twenty years have passed since OEDIPUS blinded himself after discovering that he had murdered his father and married his mother. During much of that time he has been wandering from town to town accompanied by his daughter, ANTIGONE. CREON, the regent of Thebes, has turned against him, as also have his two sons who are now contending for the throne.

OEDIPUS is about sixty-five but looks much older. Gaunt, white-haired, dressed in rags (with a beggar's wallet) and leaning on ANTIGONE, he slowly climbs the rocky path that leads to the edge of a wood, where the statue of a hero on a horse can be discerned among the trees. It is early afternoon in April.

Oedipus at Colonus

>>

PROLOGUE

OEDIPUS: I am blind and old, Antigone, my child, what
place, what people have we come to now?
And who today will dole out charity to
Oedipus the vagabond?
It's little that I ask and I make do with less.
Patience is what I've learnt from pain;
from pain and time and my own royalty.

But, child, do you see any place to sit—some
spot in public ground or sacred grove?
There set me down
just until we've found out where we are.
For we are only wanderers and must ask
advice of citizens and do as they direct.

ANTIGONE: [*Gazes across the plain towards Athens*]
Father, poor wayworn Oedipus,
the walls and turrets of the town,
as far as I can see,
are still a long way off,
but where we are is clearly consecrated
ground:
luxuriant in laurel, olive, vine,
and deep in song of nightingales.
So rest yourself upon this boulder here.
You've come too long a way for an old man.

OEDIPUS: Yes, help me down: look after the blind old
man.

ANTIGONE: If time can teach, I need no lessons there.
[*She leads him to a seat inside the grove*]

87

≪≪≪≪≪≪≪≪≪≪≪≪≪≪≪≪≪≪≪≪≪≪≪≪≪≪≪≪≪

OEDIPUS: Now tell me if you can: where have we come
to?

ANTIGONE: Well, I know it's Athens—but this spot . . .

OEDIPUS: Yes, *that* we know from every passer-by.

ANTIGONE: Then shall I go and ask what the place is
called?

OEDIPUS: Do child—if there's any sign of life.

ANTIGONE: O, but there must be!—yes, I think I needn't
go—
I see a man approaching.

OEDIPUS: Is he coming this way? Coming towards us?

ANTIGONE: He's almost on us. Quick, you speak, Father—
here he is.

[*Enter a* COUNTRYMAN *of Colonus*]

OEDIPUS: Excuse me, sir, my daughter here
whose eyes are mine as they are hers,
tells me you are passing by,
in time, I'm sure, to solve our doubts and
tell us——

COUNTRYMAN: Now, before you start your questioning
come off that seat. You're tresspassing
on holy ground.

OEDIPUS: Holy ground? What god is sacred here?

COUNTRYMAN: It's untouchable—not to be inhabited—
domain of most stern goddesses:
daughters of Earth and Darkness.

OEDIPUS: But what solemn titles should I give them in
my prayers?

COUNTRYMAN: The All-seeing Eumenides or Kindly Ones,
we call them here;
in other places no doubt graced by other
names.

OEDIPUS: Then may they welcome me, their suppliant,
for I shall never set my foot outside this
haven here.

COUNTRYMAN: What does this mean?

OEDIPUS: A sign—my fate and covenant.

COUNTRYMAN: Far be it from me, sir, to remove you.
I must tell the city first and have instruc-
tions.

OEDIPUS: Meanwhile, good stranger, for the love of
God,
don't disappoint a wretched traveler—answer me.

COUNTRYMAN: Ask. I shall not disappoint you.

OEDIPUS: What is this region that I've come into?

COUNTRYMAN: Let me tell you everything I know:
this whole place is sacred—Great Poseidon holds it.
Prometheus the Titan who bore fire is
present here.
The very spot you occupy is called,
"The Brazen Threshold" of this realm,
the "Rock of Athens."
That horseman there who rides above the
fields
is called "Colonus"—
origin and lord of all this clan.
Believe me, Stranger,
though they are not sung about,
these things make living music here.

OEDIPUS: But does this region really have inhabitants?

COUNTRYMAN: Of course, and called after their horseman
hero there.

OEDIPUS: But who governs them? Or do they rule themselves?

COUNTRYMAN: These parts are ruled from Athens by a
king.

OEDIPUS: Whose very word holds sway? Then who is
he?

COUNTRYMAN: His name is Theseus, the son of Aegeus
before him.

OEDIPUS: Then, could a messenger from among you go
to him?

‹‹

COUNTRYMAN: With a message, or inviting him to come?

OEDIPUS: To say, "a little favor wins a great reward."

COUNTRYMAN: Great reward? From one who cannot see?

OEDIPUS: Ah, there shall be sight in every word I say!

COUNTRYMAN: Listen, friend: I'm out to help.

You are obviously well-born, though down
in luck.

Stay where you are—exactly where I found
you—

while I go and tell the local people (not
the townsmen) this.

Let *them* decide whether you are to stay
or go.

[*The* COUNTRYMAN *hurries off*]

OEDIPUS: Daughter, has the stranger gone?

ANTIGONE: Gone, Father. Be at ease.

Say anything you like—
there's no one here but me.

[OEDIPUS *prays*]

OEDIPUS: Good Mistresses of terrifying face,
see me on this threshold of the land
bending knees before your throne.

Harden not your hearts against me or Apollo.

For even when he told my doom
he foretold this rest for me—after long
years:

how I should reach my journey's end
when I found a shelter at the seat of you
the dreaded Holy Ones—

there to close my life of sorrows;

how this sojourn would engender blessings
for my hosts

but curses on the people who had sent me
out and banished me.

Certain signs, he said, would warn me of
these things:

earthquakes, thunder, lightning from Zeus.

I realize now it was from you—

some inspiration gently pulled my steps
              towards this grove.
How otherwise could I at my first coming
              here
  have wandered into you
    (I, the sober, meeting you, the wineless
              ones)
  to sit upon this holy seat not made with
              human hands?
Therefore, you kind divinities,
  in fulfillment of Apollo's prophecies,
  grant me here to reach my term at last,
  some rounding off of life:
  not let me be unworth the grace of your
              dismissal,
  not let my servitude go on and on to man-
              kind's worst disaster.
Hearken to my prayer, sweet daughters of
              the ancient night!
Hearken to me, Athens—called city of great
              Pallas—
  ah, blessed of cities!
Pity this poor remnant, Oedipus,
  the ghost of what he was—a man.

ANTIGONE: Quiet, Father. Some elderly men approach
          spying out your resting place.

OEDIPUS: Yes, quiet, I'll be quiet.
          And you—hurry me from off this path into
                  the grove
          just until I hear what it is they'll say.
          Let's be informed, at least, before we act.

          [OEDIPUS *and* ANTIGONE *retreat into the grove*]

CHORAL DIALOGUE

[*Enter the* CHORUS *of the elders of Colonus. They
search among the bushes and behind the rocks
and trees, meanwhile uttering severally*]:

<<<<<<<<<<<<<<<<<<<<<<<<<<<<<<<<<<<<<<<<<<<<<<

Look for him? Who is it? Where
   can he lurk? Where has he bolted?
      Sacrilege! Sacrilege!

Comb the ground, strain your eyes
   search him out everywhere.
      Vagabond! Some aged vagabond.

No man from here! Or else
   he'd not push his way
      into this virgin plot

Of the unaffrontable maidens?
   Whose very name sends shivers.
      Whom we pass with eyes averted

Mouthing our speechless orisons
   in mute devotion.

But now,
   a sacrilegious rogue
      they say is somewhere.

And I've covered the grove on every side
   but still I cannot discover
      where he is? Where
         within the holy thicket.

              [OEDIPUS, *with* ANTIGONE, *steps*
                from behind the trees]

OEDIPUS: Here—*I* am the man
        and my eyes are my ears
        as they say of the blind.

CHORUS: Ah, sorry sight!
        And sorry sound!

OEDIPUS: Listen please,
        I am no criminal.

CHORUS: Zeus defend us!
        Who could the old man be?

OEDIPUS: Not the most blessed
        good guardians of the land
        as you can see.
        For who would borrow eyes to walk
        or lean his weight on weakness?

CHORUS: O sad,
 a man born blind!
And old as well as eyeless!
You shall not add
 if I can help
 a curse upon your sorrow.

 Trespasser, you trespass!
You go too near
 that sward of silent dell
 where the chaliced water
 blends in the stream
 of water mixed with honey.

 Stranger beset, beware!
Come away, come down:
 there is a gulf between us;
 can you hear us—you
 unhappy wanderer!
If it's speech you want
 step down from the sacred close
 and speak where it is valid.
Till then not at all!

OEDIPUS: *[Still standing within the enclosure*
          of the grove]

 My daughter, what are we to think?

ANTIGONE: Do as *they* do, Father.
 We must yield and listen.

OEDIPUS: Your hand then—come.

ANTIGONE: There, you have it.

OEDIPUS: Good friends I am breaking cover
You must not violate my trust.

CHORUS: Never fear, old man,
 No one will dislodge you—
 Not against your will.

OEDIPUS: *[Takes a step forward out of the grove]*
 Further?

CHORUS: Come still further.

OEDIPUS:	*[Takes another step]*
	Further?
CHORUS:	Lead him, girl—
	You understand
ANTIGONE:	Come, Father, come!
	Let your blind steps follow.
CHORUS:	Poor harassed foreigner on foreign soil
	Learn to hate what we hate
	And reverence what we love.
OEDIPUS:	Then lead me on, my child,
	Down the path of piety
	To where we can converse.
	There is no sense to struggle.

[He advances onto a platform of rock at the edge of the grove]

CHORUS:	There. You need not go beyond that ledge of rock.
OEDIPUS:	This far?
CHORUS:	That is far enough
	Do you hear!
OEDIPUS:	May I sit?
CHORUS:	Yes, sit to the side of that slab of rock.
ANTIGONE:	Father, this is my part.
	Take a quiet step now . . .
OEDIPUS:	Dear me!
ANTIGONE:	Step with me.
	Lean on my loving arm.
OEDIPUS:	O, the helplessness of blindness!

[ANTIGONE helps him down onto the rock]

CHORUS:	Sad sir, now you are at ease
	Tell us who you are,
	What prompts this weary pilgrimage?
	What country are you from?
OEDIPUS:	*[Alarmed]*
	Friends, I am displaced from home. I beg
	you not to . . .

CHORUS:	Yes, not to what, old man?
OEDIPUS:	Not to . . . to . . . O please! . . . To ask me who I am, Not to press and probe.
CHORUS:	Why, what is it?
OEDIPUS:	A frightening origin.
CHORUS:	Tell it.
OEDIPUS:	[*Turns to* ANTIGONE] O, my child, what can I tell them?
CHORUS:	Sir, your ancestry? Your father's name?
OEDIPUS:	O God! What shall I do, Antigone?
ANTIGONE:	Tell them. Since you've gone so far already.
OEDIPUS:	All right I'll say it. There is no way to hide it.
CHORUS:	You linger long, you two—more speed!
OEDIPUS:	You know a certain son of Laius? . . . O!
CHORUS:	Of course, we know!
OEDIPUS:	From the line of Labdacus?
CHORUS:	Great God!
OEDIPUS:	And the fallen Oedipus?
CHORUS:	What! That man is you?
OEDIPUS:	Wait, listen——
CHORUS:	O monstrous! Monstrous!
OEDIPUS:	Now it's hopeless!
CHORUS:	Monstrous!
OEDIPUS:	O daughter, what is going to happen now?
CHORUS:	Out with you! Away and leave our land!
OEDIPUS:	But you promised! You will redeem your promise?
CHORUS:	Justice does not punish man For hitting back if first he's wronged. Now we're playing trick for tricking, Paying back with pain for pleasure. Dislodge yourself. At once get moving. Skip our country, go, lest later Something fastens on our city.

ANTIGONE: O, sirs, you gentle men of pious intent,
             If my father's plight has failed to move you,
             With those heinous stories (not his doing),
                 Be kind at least to me a suppliant
                 Supplicating for my father,
             Beseeching with my eyes (for his) to yours
                 (As if indeed I almost were your daugh-
                                                      ter)
                 For a beaten man who needs some
                                               mercy.
             We're in your power now as in a god's—

             Come be gracious far beyond our hoping.
             I'll plead by all your dearest roots to life:
             Child and wife, or deity and treasure.
             Think: there never was a human being
             Who if a god should lead found hope in
                                               fleeing.

                         [*End of Choral dialogue*]

                         FIRST EPISODE

CHORUS: Daughter of Oedipus, of course we pity you,
                 just as we pity him for what he suffers;
                 but we dare not risk divine displeasure
                 and go beyond what we've said already.

OEDIPUS: Then, where has fame and where has reputa-
                                               tion gone
                 if this be Athens that most pious city?
             Sanctuary of the lost, savior of the oppressed,
                 unique in both! What good are they
                 when you tear me from my seat of stone
                 to cast me headlong from the land?
             And all because you've merely heard my
                                               name!

             O yes, it's not myself you fear,
                 not what I've done,
                 for what I've done is simply suffer . . .

if I may touch upon that story
        of my mother and my father,
which I know is what so frightens you.

And yet, how was I the sinner?
I provoked to self-defense in such a way
    that even had I acted with full knowledge,
    even then, it never could be called a sin.
As it was, where I went I went
    all ignorant towards a doom too known
    to those who planned it.

Therefore, good sirs, I ask you by the gods,
    since you have moved me from my seat,
        protect me.
Do not say you reverence heaven
    then do nothing but neglect what heaven
        says.
Think instead that God's eyes see the just
    and God's eyes see the unjust too;
    that on this earth
    no flight will save the wicked man.
By God's grace then let nothing cloud
    the glorious name of Athens.

You accepted me a suppliant and gave a
        pledge;
    now rescue me and guard me to the end.
And when you look into my ruined eyes
    do not look with scorn.
I am a dedicated man, a holy man,
    and come with graces in my hands,
    graces for this people.
And when your prince shall come,
    whoever be your prince,
    then shall everything be told and all made
        plain.
But in that space between do nothing wrong.

CHORUS: Old man, these words must make us think.
These solemn arguments have weight.
Let authority decide. I am content.

OEDIPUS: And where, sirs, does the authority of this realm reside?

CHORUS: With Theseus at the capital his father's city.
The scout who sent us here has gone for him.

OEDIPUS: What hope is there that he will come?
Why should he trouble with a blind old man?

CHORUS: Certainly he will come—once he hears your name.

OEDIPUS: But there's been no messenger to tell him that.

CHORUS: This road is long and travelers talk.
He will hear your name and he will come.
For every region of the earth has heard your name, old man.

The instant that it hits his ears
he will leap up from his recreation and his ease

and hurry here.

OEDIPUS: Then may his coming mean rewards:
for myself and for his city.
Ah, is goodness not its own reward?

ANTIGONE: Great heavens, I am speechless!
Father what can I think?

OEDIPUS: Antigone, child—what is it?

ANTIGONE: A woman's coming straight for us upon a colt—

an Etnan thoroughbred.
She has a broad Thessalian hat upon her head

to shade her from the sun.
I'm at a loss! Is it she, or isn't it?
Is my fancy playing tricks? . . .
But it must be . . .
yes, her eyes are flashing welcomes now.
She's almost on us. She is signaling—
of course . . . it is . . . no one but our own Ismene.

OEDIPUS: What are you saying, child?

ANTIGONE: Why that your daughter and my sister's here.
It's true. Her own voice will tell you.

[ISMENE, *accompanied by a single servant,
advances and throws her arms around* OED-
IPUS *and* ANTIGONE]

ISMENE: O Father! Sister!
Names so sweet to hear!
First I could not find you,
    now I cannot see you through my tears.

OEDIPUS: Daughter—you?

ISMENE: Poor dear Father!

OEDIPUS: Daughter—really you?

ISMENE: It was not easy.

OEDIPUS: Touch me, child.

ISMENE: A hand for each of you.

OEDIPUS: Ah! Blood of my blood and sisters.

ISMENE: The stricken ones.

OEDIPUS: Yes, she and I.

ISMENE: With me the third in sorrow.

OEDIPUS: But, daughter, why have you come?

ISMENE: Out of concern for you, Father.

OEDIPUS: Out of longing?

ISMENE: Yes, and to bring you news.
I could only trust myself and this last loyal
               servant here.

OEDIPUS: But those young men your brothers, where
                 are they?

ISMENE: Just where they are—in the thick of trouble.

OEDIPUS: O what miserable and perfect copies
    have they grown to be of Egyptian ways!
For there the men sit at home and weave
    while their wives go out to win the daily
                 bread.

<<<<<<<<<<<<<<<<<<<<<<<<<<<<<<<<<<<<<<

Just so your brothers, who should be
   the very ones to take this task upon them.
Instead they sit at home like girls and keep
                    the house,
   leaving the two of you to face my troubles.

Antigone, here,
   ever since she left the nursery and became
                a woman,
   has been with me as guide and old man's
                nurse—
   unhappy child—
   steering me through dreary wanderings;
   often roaming through the tangled woods
   barefoot and hungry;
   often soaked by rain and scorched by sun,
   never regretting all she missed at home,
   so long as her father was provided for.
And you, my daughter,
   once you used to sally forth
   slipping past the Theban sentinels
   with all the news of oracles about your
                father:
   you were my faithful spy
   when I was driven from the land.

But, Ismene, what new message do you bring
                your father?
What new mission made you leave your
                home?
You are not empty-handed—that I know;
   you've brought me something—something
                I can fear.

ISMENE: I went through fire and water, Father,
   trying to find out where you were
   but let that pass.
I have no desire to suffer twice,
   in reality and then in retrospect.

The trouble now is those two sons of yours.
That is what I've come to tell you of.

> They were content at first to leave the throne
> to Creon
> and keep the city free from every taint.
> For they were calm then
> realizing how the ancient family curse
> has dogged our line.

> But now they are possessed:
> some god, some pride, some jealousy,
> has gripped them with a thrice-insensate
> will
> to grasp at rule and royal power.
> The stripling younger brother has snatched
> the throne
> from the elder Polyneices—
> driven him from Thebes.
> And he, we hear from every source,
> has fled to hill-protected Argos,
> adds marriage to diplomacy and military
> alliances,
> says that Argos means to take her seat with
> honor on Theban plain
> or lift it to the skies in glorious attempt.

> This is no fiction, Father, but the agonizing
> truth.
> How far the gods will go before they let some
> mercy
> fall on you—I cannot think.

OEDIPUS: Ah! Did you think that any glances of the
gods
could ever be a glance to save me?

ISMENE: Yes, Father, that I hoped—precisely that!
There've been new oracles.

OEDIPUS: My child, what kind of oracles?
What have they said?

ISMENE: That soon the men from Thebes will find you
precious,
with a benediction on your life and death.

OEDIPUS: O who could find me wholesome—one such
as I?

ISMENE: There's power in you, so they say—
power engendered for them.

OEDIPUS: Ha! When I am nothing, then am I a man!

ISMENE: The gods now bear you up. Before they cast
you down.

OEDIPUS: So—an old man on a pedestal?—his youth in
ruins!

ISMENE: Nevertheless, you ought to know
that Creon's on his way to see if he can
use you—
and sooner now than later.

OEDIPUS: To use me, daughter? How?

ISMENE: Plant you on the frontier of Thebes, but not
inside:
within their reach, of course, but not within their sight.

OEDIPUS: On the threshold, then?
What use is that?

ISMENE: There's a curse upon your tomb if it is
wronged.

OEDIPUS: They needed neither god nor oracle to tell
them that.

ISMENE: And so they want to keep you somewhere
near,
not set you up in your own right.

OEDIPUS: And when I die, to bury me in Theban dust?

ISMENE: No, Father, no: you spilled your father's
blood.

OEDIPUS: Then I'll not fall into their hands—no, never!

ISMENE: And this, one day, will be a blow that strikes
at Thebes.

OEDIPUS: How child? How do you construe events?

ISMENE: Your wrath will overwhelm them when they
come to stand beside your tomb.

OEDIPUS:	Who told you, child? Are you repeating what you heard?
ISMENE:	Pilgrims told me from the very hearth of Delphi.
OEDIPUS:	And Apollo really said these things of me?
ISMENE:	So those men avowed on their return to Thebes.
OEDIPUS:	Has either of my sons heard this?
ISMENE:	Both of them, together; both taking it to heart.
OEDIPUS:	Scoundrels! So they knew it! Coveted my presence less than they coveted a crown.
ISMENE:	It hurts to hear you say it—but I must.
OEDIPUS:	O you gods!

Tread not down this blaze of coming battle
    but give me power to say
      what the end shall be when spear shall beat on spear
    in this incipient struggle.
Then shall the one who now enjoys the scepter and the
    throne no more remain,
    the recent exile not return.

I was their father,
    thrust out from fatherland in full disgrace.
They did not rescue or defend me.
No, they watched me harried from my home—
    my banishment proclaimed.
And if you say that such was then my wish,
    granted by the city—apt and opportune—
    I answer: 'No!'
On that first day I wished it, yes,
    death was sweet—my soul on fire—
    ah! death by stoning,
      but no man was found to further that desire.

ᕯᕯᕯᕯᕯᕯᕯᕯᕯᕯᕯᕯᕯᕯᕯᕯᕯᕯᕯᕯᕯᕯᕯᕯᕯᕯᕯᕯᕯᕯᕯᕯᕯᕯᕯᕯᕯᕯ

In time my madness mellowed.
I began to think my rage had plunged too
far,
my chastisement excessive for my sins.
And then the city—city, mark you, after all
this time—
had me thrust and hurtled out of Thebes.

Then, they could have helped—
those their father's sons, my boys—
then they could have stirred themselves.
They could. They did not do a thing.
For lack of a little word from them
I was cast out
to drag away my life in wandering penury.

My daily bread, safe guidance and devoted
care,
everything within a woman's power to
give—
these I owe to my two daughters here.
Their brothers sold their father for a throne.
exchanged him for a scepter and a realm.

No, *I'll* not help them in their war
and the crown of Thebes will prove to be
their bane.
That much Ismene's oracles make clear
now that I match them with those olden
oracles
Apollo made me once and now at last ful-
fills.

So let them send a Creon to search me out;
or any other potentate from Thebes.
With your support, my friends,
and by the grace of the Holy Ones who
here abide,
I'll be this city's champion and the scourge
of all my enemies.

CHORUS: Certainly, Oedipus, you deserve our sympa-
thies—

>>

you and your two daughters here.
And now that you add the champion weight
of your great name
I am more than ready to give you good
advice.

OEDIPUS: Spoken like a friend! And I'll do all you say.

CHORUS: Then, make amends at once to these deities
whose terrain you have trespassed on
since first coming here.

OEDIPUS: By what ritual, friends? Tell me that.

CHORUS: Well, first, from a spring of living waters
fetch
in washed and holy hands the ceremonial
cup.

OEDIPUS: And when I've fetched this living crystal
cup?

CHORUS: You'll find some bowls there of delicate design;
crown their double handles,
put wreaths along their brims.

OEDIPUS: What kind of wreaths? Olive sprigs or wool?

CHORUS: A ewe-lamb's fleece all freshly shorn.

OEDIPUS: Good. And then? . . . How do I complete
the rite?

CHORUS: Pour out your offering, with your face towards the dawn.

OEDIPUS: Pouring from those vessels that you spoke of?

CHORUS: Yes, in three libations: emptying the last
completely.

OEDIPUS: And tell me please: this last,
what should it be filled with?

CHORUS: Water mixed with honey; no drop of wine.

OEDIPUS: And when the green-dark ground has drunk
it up?

CHORUS: Then with your hands—both hands—
          lay thrice nine sprays of olive on it,
          praying as you do so.

OEDIPUS: Ah! the prayer—tell me that.

CHORUS: The prayer is to those we call the Kindly
                                            Ones—
          Eumenides—
          that they be kind and save the suppliant.
          Make that your prayer; or someone make it
                                            for you.
          Whisper it and do not cry it out.
          Then leave. Do not turn back.
          This once accomplished, I am prepared to
                                            stand by you,
          otherwise, Stranger, I should be afraid.

OEDIPUS: My daughters, are you listening to these gen-
                                            tlemen who live here?

ANTIGONE: Father, we have heard. Tell us what you
                                            want.

OEDIPUS: *I* cannot go. I am too weak and blind—
          my double disability.
          Will one of you two do it?
          A single person pure of heart, I think,
          can make atonement for a thousand sin-
                                            ners.
          Now do it with dispatch. But do not leave me
                                            all alone.
          I am not strong enough to get along without
                                            a helping hand.

ISMENE: Then I shall perform the rite, if you will tell
                                            me where—
          that I must know.

CHORUS: Beyond the copse, girl.
          A guardian there will tell you anything you
                                            want to know.

ISMENE: To my task, then.
          Antigone, you look after Father here.

No trouble's too much trouble taken for a
parent.

[ISMENE *enters the grove. The* CHORUS
turns to OEDIPUS]

SECOND CHORAL DIALOGUE

Strophe I

CHORUS: Stranger, it hurts
    to stir up the memories
      Time has let slumber
        yet longing compels me to——

OEDIPUS: What now?

CHORUS: ——Hear of the agony
    you have contended with
      so unassuageable.

OEDIPUS: For hospitality's sake, my friends,
    do not uncover my shame.

CHORUS: Which is known the world over
    and in no wise abates;
      so come—let us have it aright, sir.

OEDIPUS: Ah! Ah!

CHORUS: Be patient, please.

OEDIPUS: Shame, O, shame!

CHORUS: Come, be kind to *us*,
as *we've* been kind to you.

Antistrophe I

OEDIPUS: Friends—so many sufferings
    suffered unwittingly!
      God is my witness
        none of it guiltily.

CHORUS: Yes, but how?

≪≪≪≪≪≪≪≪≪≪≪≪≪≪≪≪≪≪≪≪≪≪≪≪≪≪≪≪≪≪≪≪≪≪

OEDIPUS: Innocent bridegroom
yoked to disaster
all in a Theban marriage.

CHORUS: Is there truth in the word that you shared
the incestuous bed of a mother?

OEDIPUS: Friends—ah!—friends,
there is death in that word;
for these maidens are mine yet . . .

CHORUS: Yes, yes? Go on.

OEDIPUS: Two   daughters,   two
curses . . .

CHORUS: God! O God!

OEDIPUS: Two fruits which have sprung
from my own mother's tree.

Strophe II

CHORUS: So these are your daughters and also your . . .

OEDIPUS: Yes, say it! . . . their own father's sisters.

CHORUS: Horrible!

OEDIPUS: Horrors in a legion
are wheeling upon me.

CHORUS: Victim!

OEDIPUS: Persecuted victim.

CHORUS: Sinner!

OEDIPUS: No sinner.

CHORUS: How's that?

OEDIPUS: A gift
was given me. Sad to have won it
and broken my heart with serving my
city.

Antistrophe II

CHORUS: Ah! broken your heart with shedding the
blood of a . . .

OEDIPUS: What is it now? What more are you after?

CHORUS: . . . a father's?

OEDIPUS: Stab! and stab again.
               wound upon wounding!

CHORUS: Killer!

OEDIPUS: I killed him, yet I can plead . . .

CHORUS: What can you?

OEDIPUS: Justice.

CHORUS: How indeed?

OEDIPUS: Listen:
               Whom I slew would have slain me,
                 so by law I am innocent—void of all malice.

[End of Choral Dialogue. THESEUS *and his train are
seen approaching. The* CHORUS *turns in his direction]*

CHORUS: But here he comes, our King,
               Theseus son of Aegeus;
               bent upon your bidding.

[Enter THESEUS *with attendants and soldiers.
                      He bows before* OEDIPUS]

THESEUS: That story widely bruited in the past—
               well known to me—
               the ensanguined murder of your sight,
               warned me it was you, Son of Laius.
             And now, hastened here by rumors,
               I can see it is.
             Your clothes and mutilated face assure me of
                                         your name,
                 and I would gently ask you, tortured
                                             Oedipus,
                 what favor you would have of me
                 —with that girl of sad expression by your
                                                 side—
                 or Athens?
             Tell me.
             For no tale of yours could make me quail:
               I was a child of exile too,

<<<<<<<<<<<<<<<<<<<<<<<<<<<<<<<<<<<<<<<<<<<<<<<<

    fighting for my life in foreign lands—
     as none so dangerously.
   Never could I turn away from any stranger
     such as you are now
     and leave him to his fate.
   For I know too well that I am only man:
     the portion of my days will be
   no more than yours tomorrow.

OEDIPUS: Theseus, in so short a speech
     all your birth's declared
     and I am freed of talking.
   My name, my father and my country—
     you've touched on all correctly.
   There's nothing left for me to say
     but tell you my desire,
     and all the tale is told.

THESEUS: Tell me that. I wait to hear it.

OEDIPUS: I come with a gift:
     this my battered body.
   No priceless vision, no,
     but the price of it is better than of beauty.

THESEUS: What can it be you think you bring so pre-
               cious?

OEDIPUS: In time you'll know. Not now perhaps.

THESEUS: And when will that time of grace be known?

OEDIPUS: When I am dead, and you have raised my
               tomb.

THESEUS: Life's last rites! You ask for that—
     with all the interval made nothing of, for-
               gotten?

OEDIPUS: Yes, for in that wish the rest is harvested.

THESEUS: You ask a little favor, then,
     compressing everything?

OEDIPUS: Perhaps . . . but not so little. Believe me—
            not so little!

THESEUS: Is something going to come between your
            sons and me?

OEDIPUS: King, they are intent to carry me off to
Thebes.

THESEUS: Which ought to please you, surely, more than
exile?

OEDIPUS: No, no—for when I wanted it they would not
have it.

THESEUS: This is foolishness to sulk in time of trouble.

OEDIPUS: Wait till you've heard me out before you
scold.

THESEUS: Proceed. I have no right to judge before I
know.

OEDIPUS: I am the victim, Theseus, of repeated and
appalling wrong.

THESEUS: You mean the family curse that haunts your
line?

OEDIPUS: No, *that* already rings in Greece's ears.

THESEUS: Then what is worse than mankind's worst
disaster?

OEDIPUS: That which abides with me.
I am driven from my country by my flesh and
blood,
I can return no more; I am a parricide.

THESEUS: What! . . . ostracized and summoned home
—in one?

OEDIPUS: A god's word makes them want me there.

THESEUS: Fearing some predicted punishment?

OEDIPUS: Forewarned of a great defeat upon this very
battlefield.

THESEUS: But there is no strife between me and them.

OEDIPUS: Son of Aegeus, gentle son,
only to the gods is given not to age or die.
All else disrupts through all-disposing Time.
Earth ebbs in strength, the body ebbs in
power.
Faith dies and faithlessness is born.

No constant friendship breathes from man
                                on man,
   or city on a city.
Soon and late in human love
   the sweet will sour, the sour will sweet to
                                love again.

Does fairweather hold between this Thebes
                                and you?

Then shall ever-pregnant Time
   teem nights on teeming days
   until a day is hatched wherein this pledge,
   this harmony, this hour,
   will break upon a spear—
   all for a useless word.

Then shall my sleeping corpse,
   cold in sepulcher,
   warm itself with draughts of their fervid
                                blood,
      if Zeus is Zeus and truth be truth
      from Zeus's son Apollo.

But I'm not one to bawl away a mystery;
   so let me stop where I began:
   take care to keep your word with me
   and then you shall not say of Oedipus
   you gave him sanctuary without reward;
   or, if you do—
   all Heaven is a fraud.

CHORUS: Sire, from the first this man has shown us
                                signs
            of being able to fulfill the things he prom-
                                ises.

THESEUS: We should be last to spurn the overtures of
                                one
            who not only shares our allies' mutual
                                rights to hospitality
            but comes before our gods with graces in
                                his hands.
          I shall reverence not repudiate his gift.

I make him citizen.
And if it please our guest to remain here
    I appoint you to look after him.
Or if he'd rather come with me . . .
    Oedipus, the choice is yours—
    your every wish is mine.

OEDIPUS: O God, be gentle to such gentleness!

THESEUS: Well, what is your will? . . . Is it to my
                                                    house?

OEDIPUS: If only that were fitting—
    but this is the spot where . . .

THESEUS: Where you must what? I shall not stop you.

OEDIPUS: . . . Crush those enemies who banished me.

THESEUS: And then will flow those blessings
    which your presence promises?

OEDIPUS: Only if you keep your word to me.

THESEUS: Never doubt it—I am one who will not fail
                                                    you.

OEDIPUS: And I'll not make you swear it like a thief.

THESEUS: You'd gain no more by that than by my
                                            common word.

[OEDIPUS *becomes anxious realizing that*
            THESEUS *is preparing to go*]

OEDIPUS: How will you proceed?

THESEUS: What is frightening you?

OEDIPUS: Men will come.

THESEUS: And mine will see to them.

OEDIPUS: But if you leave me?

THESEUS: *I'll* know what to do.

OEDIPUS: My heart is full of fear.

THESEUS: And mine is steady.

OEDIPUS: But, the threats . . . You do not know . . .

THESEUS: I know that no one's going to kidnap you
    against my will.

Often bluff and bluster, threat and counter-
threat,
    can bully reason for a time,
    but when the mind reseats itself
    disquiet vanishes.
These people who have shouted lustily
    for your return
    will find, I trust, a long and ruffled passage
here.
Have confidence! Apart from all my prom-
ises,
    has not Apollo charge of you within this
ground?
And when I'm gone my name's enough to
keep you sound.

    [THESEUS *leaves with his train. The*
    CHORUS *faces the audience*]

CHORAL ODE

Strophe I

Stranger, here
Is the land of the horse
Earth's fairest home
This silver hill Colonus.

Here the nightingale
Spills perennial sound
Lucent through the evergreen.

Here the wine-deep ivies creep
Through the god's untrodden bower
Heavy with the laurel berry.

Here there is a sunless quiet
Riven by no storm.
Here the corybantic foot
Of Bacchus beats
Tossing with the nymphs who nursed him.

Antistrophe I

The narcissus
That drinks sky's dew
Here lifts its day-by-day-born
Curls, the diadem
Of ancient goddesses.

The crocus casts his saffron glance
And unparched Cephisus each day
Wanders out from sleepless springs
Fingering his stainless way
Out among the gentle breasts
Of hills and dales
Swelling with fecundity.

Strophe II

Not in Asia
Never in Pelops
(Great Dorian island)
Was heard the like of what I sing:
A tree indomitable
Self-engendered
Challenge to the spears of armies
Lush in Athens
Sap of children—
Olive, the moon green olive.
No youth in lustihood
Shall ravish her
And not abiding age.
The sleepless eye of Zeus is on her
Athena's gaze—cerulean.

Antistrophe II

Add praise on praise,
Our Mother-city's
Prize and godgift:
Prowess in horses
Prowess in stallions
Prowess at sea.

<<<<<<<<<<<<<<<<<<<<<<<<<<<<<<<<<<<<<<<<

> You Poseidon son of Cronus
> Sat her high
> Rode her down
> These roads displaying
> How the bit and bridle
> Breaks the stamping charger
> How the oarblade
> Sleekly stroking
> Cuts the brine behind
> The hundred-footed Nereids.

SECOND EPISODE

[ANTIGONE *is seen closely observing
the approach of someone*]

ANTIGONE: O you so lauded land—the hour has come
                for you to make words shine with deeds.

OEDIPUS: Child, what now?

ANTIGONE: Creon is coming;
                and, Father, not alone.

OEDIPUS: You generous elders,
                now is the time to prove
                the limits of your sanctuary.

CHORUS: Courage! Proof you'll have.
                Though I be old,
                my country's strength is young.

                    [CREON *arrives at the head of
                        an escort of guards*]

CREON: Sirs, you worthy men of Attica,
                I see some apprehension in your eyes at
                                my approach.
            Do not recoil. Do not be ready with abuse.
            An old man against a mighty state?—
                mighty if there ever was in Greece!—No.
            My mission is to plead with that old man
                to return with me to Theban territory.
            I am no private emissary—ah no!—
                but a nation's full ambassador.

It was my lot as this man's relative
    to bear the crushing load of his estate
    as no one else in Thebes.

Do you hear me, Oedipus?
Come home you woebegotten man!
Everyone in Thebes is rightly calling for you;
    I most of all, yes, I,
    who'd be a brute indeed
    did I not weep to see an old man suffer so:
drifting endlessly, unknown, a vagabond,
    a girl his single prop—
    and she poor thwarted creature
    fallen lower than *I* could ever dream she'd
                fall,
    the muffled light of squalidness and dark,
    well ripe for weddings but unwed, and
              waiting . . . ah!
    for some thick-fisted yokel's snatch.

A disgrace?
Yes, we are all disgraced:
    I point at you and me and all of Thebes.
And who can cover up what so emblazons
              forth?
O listen Oedipus, by all your father's gods,
    you, you can hide it—now.
Consent to go back home, your own ances-
             tral city.
Say good-bye to Athens, kind as she has been.
Home comes first,
    the place of long-gone cradlehood.

OEDIPUS: You bold-faced battening villain,
    battening on the shadow of a claim
    and twisting it to specious right!
You would entrap me—eh?—a second time;
    drag me back in hateful coils?

Once there was an agony that made me turn
              against myself
    and beg aloud for banishment.

‹‹

Then it did not fit your pleasure—did it?—
 to fit yourself to mine.
But when my overbrimming passion had
         gone down
 and home's four walls were sweet,
 then you had me routed out and thrown
          away;
 fine affection *that* for family ties!

And now, again, the moment you descry
 a city and her sons are being kind,
 you want to pluck me out,
 your barbed designs wrapped up in words
         of wool.

Who ever heard of joy or love by force?
You're like a man who when he's asked,
 spurns all requests,
 gives nothing,
 will not lift a finger for you,
 but when one's had one's heart's desire
 wants to push that grace upon you—
 now a grace no longer.

Rather barren of delight that gift, don't you
         think?

Yet that precisely is the thing you proffer me:
 so fair in form, so hollow in reality.

Therefore, let me shout it out to these,
 and let them gaze on your duplicity.
You come to fetch me—
 home? Ah no!
You come to plant me on your doorstep—
 a talisman to ward away the onslaughts
         Attica will launch.
That wish you'll never have,
 but this you will:
 my curse forever on your land,
 and for my sons this sole realm and heri-
         tage—
right and room enough to die.

Ha! I'd say my forecast for the fate of Thebes
 is more informed than yours.
O more—so much the more reliable!
It stems from Phoebus and from Zeus.
Yours is from a counterfeiting tongue—
 a tongue all double-edged and whetted to
          deceit.
But yours, you'll find, will reap more suffer-
        ing than success.
However, since I cannot make you see this—
          go!
And leave us here to live
 a life of sorrows, yes,
 but bearable to one resigned to it.

CREON: This speech of yours, this parceling of events,
 whom do you think it hurts,
 you or me?

OEDIPUS: What care I,
 so long as you fail
 as thoroughly to dupe these people here
 as you have failed with me.

CREON: Silly obdurate man!
You want the world to see
 how even time denied you wit—
 gone down to dotage in disgrace?

OEDIPUS: Such a clever tongue!
I never knew an honest man
 who could dissertate at random so.

CREON: Dissertations do not always hit their mark.

OEDIPUS: But yours, of course, hit the bull's-eye
        straight!

CREON: Hardly! Aimed at such a genius.

OEDIPUS: Go! I speak for us all.
I do not want your prying eyes around my
       future home.

CREON: Then, I address myself to these people here,
       not you.

	As to you, this repudiation of your friends, if ever I take you——
OEDIPUS:	What—take by force? With these my allies looking on?
CREON:	You wait! I'll make you wince another way.
OEDIPUS:	What way? I call your big-mouthed bluff.
CREON:	One of your two daughters I've just seized and sent away. I'll remove the other now.
OEDIPUS:	O, O!
CREON:	Your 'O's' will soon increase in strength.
OEDIPUS:	Friends, my friends— what will you do? Will you forsake me? Will you not drive this impious man away?
CHORUS:	Sir, off with you! This behavior is not right— not right what you have done.
CREON:	*[To his guards]* Now's the time to take that girl. Seize her if she won't come quietly. *[The guards advance on* ANTIGONE*]*
ANTIGONE:	Help! Is there no escape? O gods! O man!
CHORUS:	What are you doing, sirrah?
CREON:	I shan't touch your man. *She* is mine.
OEDIPUS:	Elders, help!
CHORUS:	Sir, you have no right.
CREON:	I have.
CHORUS:	What right?
CREON:	To take what's mine. *[*CREON *lays hands on* ANTIGONE*]*

[The following lines form a strophe in the Greek which is answered later by an antistrophe when CREON *attacks* OEDIPUS *himself. This short choral interlude serves both to sustain the excitement and yet to relieve the tension.]*

Strophe

OEDIPUS: O no!
       Athens, help!

CHORUS: How dare you, Stranger!
                *[*CHORUS *approaches menacingly]*
       Let her go—
       Or you must run the danger
       Of our attack.

CREON: Stand back!

CHORUS: Not until you yield.

CREON: Then it's Thebes and Athens on the battle-
                              field.

[End of strophe]

OEDIPUS: Ah! My words come true!

CHORUS: *[Spoken to* CREON's *guards]*
       Let loose the girl, or you——

CREON: Mind your own authority.

CHORUS: I'm telling you to let her free.

CREON: I'm telling you to go away.

CHORUS: Colonians, to the rescue! Help!
       The State itself at bay!
       The State manhandled, help!

ANTIGONE: Friends! Friends! They're dragging me away!

OEDIPUS: My child, where are you?

ANTIGONE: They're pulling me away.

OEDIPUS: Child—a hand.

ANTIGONE: I cannot move.

CREON: Get on with her.   *[To his guards]*

OEDIPUS: O done, undone, I'm done away with!

> [*The guards hustle* ANTIGONE *off.*
> CREON *turns to* OEDIPUS *with a sneer*]

CREON: At least you won't go hobbling through your
life

> with those two crutches any more!
> If that's the kind of triumph you want—
> trampling over friends and country,
> those whose mandate, I though King,
> am trying to carry out—
> then have that triumph.
> In time, I think, you'll learn
> what little good you've done yourself
> now or ever,
> flying into tempers at your friends:
> cursed tempers that have ruined you.

> [CREON *begins to walk away behind his men*]

CHORUS: Hold there, Stranger!

> [*The* CHORUS *makes an effort to
> lay hold of* CREON]

CREON: Hands off, I say!

CHORUS: Not until you give back those two girls.

CREON: Persist and you'll present my city with an
even

> greater prize;
> for I shall lay my hands on more than
> these.

> [*He wheels round on* OEDIPUS]

CHORUS: Whatever next?

CREON: Him. He's mine.

CHORUS: Braggart!

CREON: Watch me do it!

CHORUS: With permission of our King, of course!

OEDIPUS: Scandalous brute—you wouldn't dare!

CREON: Silence, you!

OEDIPUS: Silence? No!
If the spirits of this place allow
I shall give vent to one more curse:
may Helios, all-seeing god of sun,
visit you and all your race
with such senility one day
as matches mine.

CREON: You see this, citizens?

OEDIPUS: They see us—you and me:
they see how you have deeds to batter
me
and I have only air to counter with.

CREON: I will not stand it more.
Old and slow and singlehanded
I'll take that man by force.

[CREON *attempts to lay hands on* OEDIPUS]

Antistrophe

[*Answering strophe on page 123*]

OEDIPUS: You'll rue it!

CHORUS: Rash man,
What makes you think that you can do it?

CREON: I can.

CHORUS: Then is Athens city most degenerate.

CREON: Where right is might the little beat the great.

OEDIPUS: Hear him?

CHORUS: Rant—God knows!

CREON: Perhaps God knows—you can't.

CHORUS: Blasphemy!

CREON: Then you'll have to bear with blasphemy.

CHORUS: Rally people! Rulers rally!
To the rescue—hurry!
These ruffians board our boundary.

[*End of antistrophe*]

[THESEUS *arrives at the head of his troop*]

THESEUS:	I heard a shout. What made you shout?
	 I was at the sea-god's altar—
	     great Poseidon's of Colonus.
	 Your panic cry arrested me at sacrifice
	     and made me hurry here
	         (too quick for comfort) . . .
	     but tell me everything.

OEDIPUS:	Ah! Gentle voice— I am worsted by a brigand.
THESEUS:	Worsted? How? Say who?

OEDIPUS:	Creon here, this creature which you see,
	     has kidnapped my two children—
	     my last and darling pair.

THESEUS:	Is this true?
OEDIPUS:	As I tell it: O most costly truth!

[THESEUS *to his men*]

THESEUS:	Quick, one of you to the altar place:
	     break up the concourse at the sacrifice,
	     and have the people gallop foot and horse
	     to the meeting of the roads before the
	                 women pass,
	     before I'm made this foreign bully's laugh-
	               ingstock.

[*A soldier is dispatched*]

[*Pointing at* CREON]

As for him,
    if I should let my anger have full sway
    to deal with him as he deserves,
    he should not leave my hands without a
              smart.

But now, we'll mete him out correction
    by the very law and measure he himself
            has brought here.

[*Addressing* CREON]

You shall not leave this country, sir,
    until those girls are back
    and stand before my eyes.

You insult us;
    you insult your very race and native land.
You push your way within this realm
    where right is loved and law is paramount
    and then proceed to sweep aside authority,
    pillaging and taking prisoners at your will
    as if you thought my city was bereft of men
    or manned by slaves
    and I a nobody.

Well, it was not Thebes that brought you up
                            to steal.
She has no predilection for a rascal brood.
Scant praise you'd have from her
    if she found you plundering me—
    yes, plundering the gods—
    carrying off poor wretched worshippers at
                            prayer.

Never could *I* so seize and snatch,
    entering territory of yours—
    not even if I had a more than royal right—
    unless whoever governed gave me leave
                            for it.
I should know how a guest behaves among
                            true citizens.

But you, you dishonor even your native land,
    so undeserving of disgrace.
Length of days has made you ripe in age
    but far from ripe in reason.

I have said it once,
    I say it once again:
    restore these girls immediately
    unless you want to make a lengthy stay here
    not quite according to your will.
This is not eulogistic talk—
    I mean it, every word.

CHORUS: Stranger—see the reputation you have
                            reaped!
            Good stock from Thebes gone wrong.

CREON: Theseus son of Aegeus,
               I never thought your city was unmanned,
               or drifting rudderless, as you suggest.
           That never prompted what I did.
           I merely thought your people could not love
                                       my family so
               that it would harbor one of them against
                                       my wish
               and welcome here
               a parricide,
               a tainted man,
               a man discovered—O the filth of it—
               both bridegroom and his mother's son.

           I took for granted that the Council of the
                                       Areopagus
               would never in its wisdom let
               roam at large such vagabonds of sin in
                                       Attica.
           Convinced of this I took him as my prize.
           And even then I might have let him go
               had he not loaded me and all my race
               with the foulest imprecations.
           I've stomached quite enough, I think,
               to justify reprisals.
           Rage, remember, knows no age till death.
           Nothing hurts the dead.

           Well, do what you will.
           Right though I am
               what headway can I make alone?
           Yes, I am old,
               but I shall strain
               to answer every plan with counterplan.

OEDIPUS: Arrant monster!
           Where do you think these insults fall—
               on my old head or yours?
           Murder, incest, and catastrophe—
               you spew the lot at me,
               and all the lot I bore in misery,

not through any choice of mine
but through some scheme of heaven,
long insensate perhaps against our house.

Examine me apart from this
and you will find no flaw to cavil at
that might have drawn me so to flaw
my family and myself.
For tell me this:
suppose the oracle had laid it down
my father through God's destiny must die
by his own hands,
could you justly put the blame on me—
a babe unborn,
not yet begotten of a father,
not yet engendered in a mother's womb?

And if when born, as born I was,
to tragedy,
I met my father in a fight,
killed him,
ignorant of what I did, to whom I did it,
can you still condemn an unwilled act?

And my mother, your own sister—
wretched man—
since you're low enough to drag her marriage in
and force me to allude to it,
I shall;
I'll not keep silent on so much
that your foul mouth has shouted out.
My mother,
yes, she was my mother—
horrible!
I did not know,
she did not know.
And to her shame
she gave me children—
children to the son whom she herself had
given.

But, one thing at least I know:
    you vituperate by choice—her and me,
    when not by choice I married her,
    and not by choice am speaking now.

Neither in this marriage then
    shall I be called to blame,
    nor in the way my father died—
    on which you harp with so much spite.

Let me ask you this, one simple thing:
    if at this moment someone should
    step up to murder you,
    would you, godly creature that you are,
    stop and say: "Excuse me, sir, are you my
                      father?"
Or would you deal with him there and then?
Ah! you love your life too much, I think.
You would attack,
    not look around to find a warrant first.

That precisely is the plight that heaven put
                    me in.
My very father's soul, come back, would not
                    say no.
But you, unscrupulous creature that you are,
    a man convinced that everything he says
                  is fit to hear—
    who bawls out every secret thing—
    you heap your slanders on me publicly,
    meanwhile making sure to bow and scrape
    before the name of Theseus,
    with compliments on how the state of
                  Athens runs.

Very well, extol them to the skies
    but don't forget,
    if there's any state that knows what true
                religion is
    that state is this.
You planned to wrest a worshipper away,
    and old man too.

You tried to capture me.
You have already captured both my daughters.

Therefore I put my case before these goddesses,
  lay siege to them in prayer,
  assail them for their help—
  to fight for me
  and manifest to you
  the quality of men that guard this realm.

CHORUS: Sire, he is an honest man:
  not a lucky man but worthy of our help.

THESEUS: Enough of talk!
The criminals are in full flight
  while we are standing still.

CREON: I am helpless, then.
What is it I must do?

THESEUS: My pleasure is that you should show the
way,
  and I shall escort you.
You yourself shall take me to wherever
  you have hidden those two missing maids.
But if your men have hustled off with them
  we shall spare ourselves the pains.
Others will give chase and hunt your soldiers
down,
  and no one will give thanks at home for
their return.

Proceed! And don't forget,
  the looter has been looted,
  the trapper's in the trap,
  and stolen goods soon spoil.

You shall lack your ally too in this affair.
O yes, I know you did not push yourself
so far
  without some help or backing.
No, you had your faith in someone
  when you made your dastardly attempt.

And I must look to it—
> not jeopardize my city for a single man.
Does this make sense
> or do I speak as emptily to you as spoke
>> those warnings once
> when first you hatched your plans?

CREON: I shall not argue with you here.
But once at home I'll have my inspirations
> too.

THESEUS: Threaten but keep moving, please.
Oedipus, stay here in peace;
> happy in the promise that I give:
> I'll have your children back
> or I'll not live.

OEDIPUS: God bless you, Theseus, for this generosity.
God bless you for your faithful care of me.
> [CREON *begins marching, followed by*
>> THESEUS *and his troop*]

SECOND CHORAL ODE

Strophe I

O to be there
When the brigands at bay
Turn to the clash
Of brass on brass
By the Pythian shore

Or the flaring sands
Of Eleusis where
The Queens of the Night
And their honey-voiced hymners
Solemnly seal
In tongues of gold
The rites of men.

Ah! I think Theseus
Springs to the fight
With presage of victory

Strong in his shout:
Soon to make safe
Two sisterly captives
Still in our land.

Antistrophe I

Or perhaps they will come
To the western plains
Near rocky Oea's
Snowblanched side:
Neck and neck in the race,
Chariots flying
Till Creon is worsted.
Might of Colonus
Might of Theseus'
Stalwart men.

Ah! Flash of the harness
Toss of the reins!
Cavalry gallops
Body of horsemen
Dear to Athena
Queen of the horse,
Dear to Poseidon
Ocean embracer
Fond son of Rhea.

Strophe II

The tussle is on
Or is it now imminent?
Beautiful hope
Telling me presently:
Maidens restored
Cornered so cruelly
Uncle so cruel.
Victory victory
Zeus win the day!
Success in the struggle
Is what I foretell.

O that my eyes
High on the fight
Were eyes of a dove
That sails down the storm
And lifts to the passing cloud.

Antistrophe II

All-seeing Zeus
All-ruling all!
Let this country's
Guardians conquer
Quarry and prize.
Grant O grant it
Your daughter too
Our lady stern
Pallas Athena.
Grant it Apollo
Hunter who
With sister chases
The light-footed moon-
Speckled deer. O come
With coupled help
For this land and people.

[*There is a pause while the strains of the
choral ode die away*]

THIRD EPISODE

[*One of the* CHORUS *reports from the lookout*]

CHORUS: Wanderer, look!
            Our watcher's forecast was not false:
              I see the girls are coming under escort.

OEDIPUS: Where, where? How could it possibly . . . ?
            [ANTIGONE *and* ISMENE *approach, followed
            by* THESEUS *and his soldiers.* ANTIGONE *is at
            first a little ahead of her sister*]

ANTIGONE: Father, father!
O I wish some god could make you see
    this princely man who has brought us back
        to you!

OEDIPUS: My child—it's you?

ANTIGONE: Yes, saved by his strong arm;
    by Theseus and his loyal men.

OEDIPUS: Daughter, come to me.
Let your father press you to his side—
    redeemed beyond all hope!

ANTIGONE: You shall; a gift we long to give.

OEDIPUS: But where—where are you?

ANTIGONE: Both hurrying towards you hand in hand.

OEDIPUS: My own sweet children!

ANTIGONE: Sweet and fond to a father.

OEDIPUS: Dear props of my life.

ANTIGONE: And partners in pain.

OEDIPUS: My darlings . . . mine again!
If I died now they would say
    he was not altogether damned;
    he had his children with him . . .
O press close to me
    each of you,
    don't let your father go.
Rest from your late roaming
    so cruel and forlorn
    and tell me in a word what happened:
    young girls need no speeches.

ANTIGONE: Father, our rescuer is here:
    you should learn it all from him.
The credit's his.
There—my speech was short!

OEDIPUS: Sir, forgive me!
I cannot welcome them enough.
My children were lost—
    now they are found,

and you are the one who brings this joy to
me.

You rescued them, no man beside.
God reward you and this blessed land,
    where more than any place on earth,
    amongst you I have found the fear of God,
    I have found fair play and honesty.
These things I recognize and pay my homage
to.

All that I have I have through you,
    and no one else.

And now, my King,
    give me your right hand
    and may I put a kiss upon your cheek?

                    [*Suddenly checks himself*]

What am I saying?
What is this invitation that I make
    to handle me a man of sorrows,
    a temple of pollution?
No, no! Never let it be!
Let my sufferings lodge with those tried
                    souls
    who must drink with me the bitter cup.
I salute you from afar.
Keep me always in your gentle care
    as until this hour you have.

THESEUS: No, Oedipus, this is nothing strange:
    your shower of words, your open heart,
                    your joy.

Of course you had to greet your children
                    first.

How could *that* fill me with dismay?
Besides, I'd rather furbish life with sparkling
                    deeds than words;
    as I have proved to you, old man,
    making perfect everything I pledged:
    presenting you with daughters both re-
                    deemed—

rescued from all threats.
As to the manner of my victory,
   why should I puff it up?
They will tell you everything.

Meanwhile, some late news has come my
   way
   and I should like your thoughts upon it.
It hardly sounds important—
   and yet it puzzles me.
There's nothing that a human being safely
   can dismiss.

OEDIPUS: What is it, son of Aegeus?
   No news of anything has come to us.

THESEUS: They say a man—
   not from Thebes and yet a relative of
   yours—
   has unexpectedly appeared;
   is prone in prayer before Poseidon's altar,
   where I was worshipping before I started
   here.

OEDIPUS: A man from where?
   And what is his petition?

THESEUS: This is all I know:
   they say he wants a word with you
   which will not cost you much.

OEDIPUS: Only a word—yet prostrate in petition?

THESEUS: They say he only wants to speak with you
   then go his way in peace.

OEDIPUS: Who is this suppliant, I wonder, at the
   shrine?

THESEUS: Think of Argos—have you any kinsman there
   who might ask a like request?

OEDIPUS: [*Alarmed*]
   O, dear friend, do not go on!

THESEUS: Why not?
   What troubles you?

OEDIPUS: Don't ask.

THESEUS: What is it? Tell me.

OEDIPUS: Your words have made me guess the sup-
                                                pliant.

THESEUS: And who is he? What mutual enemy?

OEDIPUS: Sire, my son:
                  my own detested son.
              There's no man's voice I'd find so poisonous.

THESEUS: But why?
              Can hearing make you go against your will—
                  his voice give actual pain?

OEDIPUS: Hate, my King, is what that voice has
                                                earned:
                  a father's hate.
              Do not press me to give way.

THESEUS: Perhaps you must . . . his supplicant role . . .
                  duty to the god. Reflect.

ANTIGONE: Father, listen to me, young though I am.
              Let the King's desire be honored to gratify
                                                the gods.

              O do it for your daughters' sakes
                  and let their brother come!
              After all, whatever pain his words may give,
                  he cannot wrench your will away.
              His voice? What damage can that do?
              Besides, it's talk that best betrays the foul
                                                design.

              He is your son.
              And even if his conduct reached the
                  heights of disrespect and wickedness,
                  Father, that would never make it right for
                                                        you
                  to strike him back.
              So let him come!

              Many a man is pricked to anger by a
                  worthless son,
                  but, listening to his friends,

>>>

is coaxed from harshness back to gentleness.
Cast your thoughts to what has been
not what is now:
the hardships sprung from father and a
mother.
Ponder these and realize
how catastrophic anger brings catastrophe.
Feed thought on that,
and those two sightless sockets once your
eyes.
Come, give way to us!
Must we special-plead for a cause so fair?
Can one whom mercy's touched
then turn his back on mercy?

OEDIPUS: Daughter,
a hard-won joy you wring from me.
Well, have it as you wish.

[*Turns to* THESEUS]

But, O my friend, that man—if he must come,
then never let my soul go down in slavery.

THESEUS: Enough! Once will do.
I need not hear it twice, old man!
Nor need I boast:
your life is safe—be sure of that—
while any god saves mine.

[THESEUS *leaves with his soldiers. The*
CHORUS *turns to the audience and prepares
it for the final scene:* OEDIPUS's *release from
life's bondage*]

THIRD CHORAL ODE

Strophe I

Where is the man who wants
More length of days
O cry it out:
There is a fool

His dawdling years
Are loaded down with cares
His joys are flown
His extra time but trickles on
He waits the Comforter
Who comes to all.
No wedding march
No dancing song
A sudden vista down stark avenues
To Hades Halls:
Then Death at last.

Antistrophe

Not to be born has no compare
But if you are
Then hurry hence
For after that there is no better blessing.
When one has watched gay youth
Pack up his gallant gear
Vexations crowd without
And worries crowd within:
Envy, discord, struggles
Shambles after battles
Till at last he too must have his turn
Of age: discredited and doddering
Disaffected and deserted age
Confined with crabbedness
And every dismal thing.

Epode

So are we senile—he and I
Lashed from the north by wintry waves
Like some spume-driven cape on every side
Lashed by our agonies those constant waves
Breaking in from the setting sun
Breaking in from the dawn
Breaking in from the glazing south
Breaking in from Polar gloom.

FOURTH EPISODE

ANTIGONE: Father, look:
I think I see our visitor approach;
he is alone. The tears are streaming from
his eyes.

OEDIPUS: Who is he?

ANTIGONE: Exactly whom we thought:
it's Polyneices who has come.

[POLYNEICES *enters, advances, then stands aghast*]

POLYNEICES: O God! What shall I do?
Sisters, sisters! Shall I pour out tears
for my own calamities
or for this sorry sight—
my poor decrepit father?
Whom here I find
jettisoned with you two in a foreign land;
arrayed in such unkind and antique filth
his own antiquity corrodes with it:
his hair above his sightless eyes
unkempt and straggling out upon the
breeze;
and, matching these, his beggar's scrip
with pittance for his wasted belly.

Ah—too late! A vision seen too late!
I pronounce that this neglect of you
convicts me as the most delinquent thing
on earth.
Yes, let me be the first to say it.
But, Father,
Zeus himself seats Mercy by his throne,
so may you seat her near you too.
We can mend all these mistakes
and not make more.

[*He pauses anxiously*]

You are silent!
Say something, Father, please.

Don't turn away from me.
Have you no reply to make?
Will you send me off in dumb contempt?
Not even tell me what upsets you so?

[He pauses again]

O you his children, you at least my sisters,
   try to move him from this rigidness so
                       mute.

I must not be dismissed in shame
   without a word
      from God's own sanctuary.

[He pauses a third time]

ANTIGONE: Tell him yourself, sad brother, what it is
                   you've come for.
Sometimes as words begin to flow
   here they strike a spark of joy
     there they fan up anger or a little tender-
                     ness,
   and anyhow give voice to what is dumb.

POLYNEICES: Then I'll speak out, for you advise me well,
   and first will make it plain:
   the god I've called upon for help
   is that very ocean-god
   from whose suppliant shrine this country's
                       king
   has raised me up and let me come here
   with safe passport to confer with you.

And therefore I would ask you gentlemen,
   my sisters here, and you my father,
   to respect my rights in this.

And now I'll tell you, Father, why I came:

I'm driven out, an exile from my land,
   because as eldest son
     I claimed my sovereign birthright to the
                       throne.
This was why Eteocles my younger brother
                   cast me out,

not by making good his claims,
nor by proof of excellence,
but by cajoling the city to his side.
All of which I am inclined to blame
upon the Fury that pursues your house.
And this the various oracles confirm.

So I went to Doric Argos;
took to wife the daughter of the King
Adrastus
and made a league
of all the famous fighters of the Pelopon-
nese—
a seven-headed army aimed at Thebes—
to die in the attempt, die gloriously,
or oust those from the realm who ousted
me.

Well then, what's my end in coming here?
Father, this:
to lay our supplications at your feet,
mine and all my allies:
who at this moment ring their seven cham-
pioned armies
round the plain of Thebes.

There's Amphiareus, the hurricane spears-
man,
first at the spear, first at the reading of
riddles.
Then the son of Oeneus: Tydeus of Aetolia.
Third comes Eteoclus, native of Argos.
Fourth, Hippomedon, sent by Talaus his
father.
Fifthly Capaneus, swearing to mow down
Thebes with fire.
Sixthly battle-hot Parthenopaeus of Arcadia
(called after Atalanta, famous virgin,
who later married and became the mother
of this stalwart boy);

And lastly, I, your son—
 or if I'm not your son
 but child of some appalling destiny—
 then, son at least in name.
I am the one who puts this fearless Argos in
        the field
 against the state of Thebes.

Father, will you listen to us all?
Listen to us for your daughters' and your
        own life's sake.
Ease the harshness of your rage against me
         now,
 who sally out to give this brother chas-
        tisement,
 the robber of my home.
If there's any truth in prophecy,
 the oracles have said that victory lies
 with those who win you to their side.

Now listen, Father, if you love our land
 of springing fountains and our Theban
        gods,
 be persuaded by my prayer.
We are banished, you and I,
 both of us are beggars.
We have to fawn on others for a home,
 you and I,
 both share a single destiny.
And yet this creature kings it in our house.
Insufferable!
He ridicules us from his cushioned pride.

If you will bless my scheme
 I'll make short shrift of him and cast him
        out.
You will be established in your house,
 and I shall be established too.
I'll make good this boast if you'll make one
        with me.
I shall not live if you'll not now agree.

CHORUS: Oedipus, don't send the man away,
    for him who sent him's sake,
    until you've had your say.

OEDIPUS: You trustees of this realm,
    since Theseus sent him here
    and asked me to reply, I will.
Nothing less would let him hear my voice.
But now he shall be graced with it
    in accents that will make all gladness go.

               [*Turns to* POLYNEICES]

Liar!
Once you held the scepter and the throne
    which your brother at this moment holds
                    in Thebes;
    and when you did you drove me out,
    drove this your father out,
    displaced me from my city.
You were the reason for these rags—
    rags that make you cry to see,
    now that you have reached rock bottom
                    too.

The season for condolences is past.
You have crushed my life beneath a weight:
    the lasting thought of you my son, as
                   murderer.
O yes, it's you that drags me down!
You expelled me.
You arranged for me to beg my daily bread.
I should not even be alive, if left to you.
But these two girls here, born to care for me,
    they preserve me; *they* look after me.
They are the ones who play a man's and not
               a woman's part.
But you—you and your brother—are no sons
               of mine.

The eye of Fate is on you now.
Her glance is mild to what it soon shall be
    if presently your armies march on Thebes.

You shall not topple down that city.
Instead you'll trip up headlong into blood,
> your brother too,
>> spattering each other.

My soul sent up these curses once,
> and now again I summon them to fight for
>> me.
Let them demonstrate to you
> how piety to parents calls,
> alien utterly from that disrespect grown
>> rank
> towards a father who begot you and was
>> blind.
My daughters did not treat me so.
Then I'll consign to curses
> your 'petitions' and your 'royal thrones,'
> if any Justice still is seated side by side
>> with Zeus
> in ancient and eternal sway.

Depart then—disappear!
Abominated bastard not my child—
> wicked of the wicked!
Carry off these curses freshly called:
> never to flatten native land beneath the
>> spear;
> never to put foot again on Argive hill and
>> dale;
> but, but, to die by brother's blow—
> that banisher of yours whom you will kill.

So do I pray.
And so do I summon the pitchy gloom of
> Tartarus
> to welcome you within a new paternal
>> home.
I summon too the holy spirits of this place.
I summon Ares the Destroyer—
> he who whirled you into hatred and col-
>> lision.

So,
  with these imprecations in your ears—
  get out!
Go publish it in Thebes.
Go tell your bellicose and trusty friends
  what honors Oedipus bequeaths his sons.

CHORUS: Polyneices,
  so you always came and went,
  never boding peace for us,
  and now again.—Go quickly!

POLYNEICES: O pitiful!
My pointless journey here.
My hopes in ruins.
My comrades all betrayed.
Pitiful, that journey's end
  to our proud marching out from Argos—
  end not utterable to one of them.
No turning back.
No halt in silent march
  towards our doom.

[*Turns to* ANTIGONE *and* ISMENE]

But you—you his little ones, my sisters—
  who have heard these father's prayers,
                these prayers of hate,
  if they should come to bear their damnéd
                fruit
  and you should ever come to Thebes again,
  O for God's love, in that blessed chance,
  do not desecrate my name
  but put me in my tomb and wind my
                cerement.
Add praise on those your praises won from
                him
  by this last tenderness.

ANTIGONE: Polyneices, please—do one thing for me.

POLYNEICES: Antigone, sweet sister, what?

ANTIGONE: Turn your army back on Argos now.
Do not destroy yourself and Thebes.

POLYNEICES: Impossible!
How could I lead my army in the field again?

ANTIGONE: Again, dear brother? What new hate should
make you?
What can ruin of your country gain?

POLYNEICES: Yes—but running from my younger brother,
mocked like this . . .

ANTIGONE: Ah! don't you see you hasten on your father's
prophecy
of duel and double death?

POLYNEICES: Of course! It's what he wants.
But I shall *not* give way.

ANTIGONE: O, I am sick at heart!
And who will follow you
once it's heard what future he has threat-
ened?

POLYNEICES: It shan't be heard. I'll never say.
Good generals do not stress their weakness
but their strength.

ANTIGONE: Your mind's made up, my brother?

[*She clutches hold of* POLYNEICES]

POLYNEICES: Yes, and do not hold me back.
There is an avenue down which I go
all shadowed by my father's prayers
and dark with Furies answering his call.
But do these obsequies for me when I am
dead,
and Zeus reward you with a brighter way.
In life there's nothing left for you to tender
me.

Now let me go. Good-bye!
You'll never gaze again into my living eye.

[*Gently releases himself from* ANTIGONE]

ANTIGONE: I'm broken utterly.

POLYNEICES: Don't cry for me.

ANTIGONE: Who would not cry to see
you my brother hurrying to die.

POLYNEICES: If *I* must die, I'll die.

ANTIGONE: No, hear me—never you!

POLYNEICES: Don't press me uselessly.

ANTIGONE: But if you're lost what's left for me?

POLYNEICES: The future is in Fortune's hands—
    one finish or another.

    My prayer for both of you is this:
      God keep you free from every pain,
      so little merited for you, as all maintain.

    [POLYNEICES *turns and abruptly strides away*]

CHORAL ODE AND DIALOGUE

Strophe I

CHORUS: So do I see fresh sorrows strike
    Fresh strokes of leaden doom
    From the old blind visitor
    Or is it Fate unfolding:
    Supernal in her workings which
    I dare not say can fail—
    Watched, ah! watched
    By never failing Time
    Shuffling fortunes from the top to bottom?

    [*The sound of thunder*]

    The sky is rift—O God!

OEDIPUS: Quick, children, O my children
    send someone if you can
    for that princely man Prince Theseus.

ANTIGONE: Father, what should make you call him now?

OEDIPUS: That clap of thunder beating down from Zeus
    beckons me to Hades Halls.
    So hurry, someone, hurry!

    [*Another peal of thunder*]

Antistrophe I

CHORUS: Louder—hear it?—crashing down
    Divine report dumbstriking sound
    Pricking up my hair with panic

≪≪≪≪≪≪≪≪≪≪≪≪≪≪≪≪≪≪≪≪≪≪≪≪≪≪≪≪≪≪≪≪≪≪≪≪≪≪

And shattering my soul.
There up again light rips the sky
O what will it engender? I
Am undone, unstrung—
That ever pregnant rush
Is fertile in its monstrous issue
   Great awful sky! Great Zeus!

[*More thunder*]

OEDIPUS: Children, children, life closes on me now:
      that too-attested end from which there is
                      no turning.

ANTIGONE: What makes you know? What signals make
                      it clear?

OEDIPUS: I am too well-aware.
    O hurry, someone, to this country's King and
                    bring him here.

[*Thunder, louder*]

Strophe II

CHORUS: Ha! Another crash!
    The air's invaded
    All our ears are riddled.
    Mercy, mercy, God of Heaven
    Come not down in darkness
    On this earth our mother.
    Clement may I find you
    My glance though fallen
    On a man that's fated.
    O deal no curses
    For those gracious glances
    But Zeus on high be kind!

OEDIPUS: Daughters, is he here yet, here?
    Shall *I* be breathing still—
      still master of my mind?

ANTIGONE: To master what? Some promised testament?

OEDIPUS: Some crowning gift bequeathed and pledged,
      return for all he served me.

[*More thunder*]

Antistrophe II

CHORUS:
Hasten, hasten, Theseus!
Son step down
Even from obeisance
At the shaded sacrifice
Deep in Poseidon's grove
And come. For you, your people,
City, are so worth
So justly worth
This stranger's thanks, his debt
Of benisons.
So hurry, King, O hurry!

[*End of Choral Ode and Dialogue*]

[*Thunder:* THESEUS *bursts in*]

THESEUS:
What! Another summons?
Guest and subjects joined in clarion call?
Thunderbolts from Zeus and cataracts of
hail . . .
all's possible when God sends such a storm.

OEDIPUS:
King, how glad I am you've come.
A god has smoothed your way to us.

THESEUS:
What news now, son of Laius?

OEDIPUS:
The balance of my life is tilting;
I must not die a debtor,
my bargain barren still
with you and with your city.

THESEUS:
What signal makes you sure the end is close?

OEDIPUS:
The gods have sent their own dispatch,
announcing to the letter every designated
sign.

THESEUS:
What signs, old man, what signs?

OEDIPUS:
This rolling thunder, rolled, this shuttled
light:
the mighty bolts of God's artillery.

THESEUS:
And I believe.
You never did foreshadow falsely.
Declare what we must do.

∢∢∢∢∢∢∢∢∢∢∢∢∢∢∢∢∢∢∢∢∢∢∢∢∢∢∢∢∢∢∢∢∢∢∢

[*With great solemnity* OEDIPUS
takes THESEUS *aside*]

OEDIPUS: Come, listen, son of Aegeus,
 I'll lay before you now a city's lasting
         treasure.
There is a place where I must die,
 and I myself, unhelped, shall walk before
         you there.
That place you must not tell to any human
         being:
 not where it lurks, nor where the region
         lies—
 if you would have a shield like a thousand
         shields,
 and a more perpetual pact than spears of
         allies.

No chart of words shall mark that mystery.
Alone you'll go: alone your memory
 shall frame it in that spot.
For not to any persons here
 not even to my daughters so beloved
 am I allowed to utter it.
You yourself must guard it always.
And when your life is drawing to its close
 divulge it to your heir alone
 and he in turn to his, and so forever.

This way you'll keep your city safe against
      the Dragon's Seed,
 though many a state attack a peaceful
         home,
 though sure be the help from heaven
 (but exceeding slow)
 against earth's godless men and men gone
         mad.
No such fate for you, good son of Aegeus.
But all of this you know without my telling
         you.

And now to that spot—God signals me.
We'll linger here no more.

[OEDIPUS's *face lights up as if he is inspired.
With slow firm steps he moves forward, calling for the others to follow*]

Come children, follow, follow this new leader—
father guiding you whom once you guided.
On, on—hands off—and let me walk my way
without a prop towards my hidden tomb:
that soil of Attica to cover me.
This way, this way—come!
For this way Hermes escorts me—
and the Mistress of the Dead.

[*Looking up into the direction of the sun*]

Ah! Good-bye, you blindfold light once light
of mine,
last vision felt in darkness.
I'll walk to Hades now and close my final
coil.

[*Turns to* THESEUS]

Most gentle friend,
heaven bless you, bless your land and
yours.
And in prosperity remember me the dead,
to have abiding blessings on your head.

[*He passes from the stage, followed by
his daughters and by* THESEUS]

FOURTH CHORAL ODE

Strophe

Dare I adore the unseen Queen
And you night's children's King?
Then Aidoneus, listen, Aidoneus:
Not in pain and lamentation shall his deathknell ring
This stranger passing down through palisades of gloom

≪≪≪≪≪≪≪≪≪≪≪≪≪≪≪≪≪≪≪≪≪≪≪≪≪≪≪≪≪≪≪≪≪≪≪≪≪≪≪

Towards those prairies of the dead
His Stygian home.
Much did he suffer
Much beyond deserts
Let the finger of God's fairness
Raise him now.

Antistrophe

Goddesses of world's deep down
And you unvanquished hound of hell
Immóbile by those gates of many guests
The untamed watcher legend says of Hades pit
And Death you son of Earth and Tartarus, I beg
That Cerberus may not molest
The path of Oedipus
Who walks towards
Those sunken meadows of the dead.
O Death, I beg, bestow on him
Eternal rest!

> [*There is a long pause and then
> a* MESSENGER *enters*]

FIFTH EPISODE

Exodos

MESSENGER: Fellow citizens,
    I could cut this story short and say:
    'Oedipus is gone,'
    but, what was done was not done shortly,
    and the story breaks away from brevity.

CHORUS: So the man of destiny is gone?

MESSENGER: Gone—
    he's left this life behind.

CHORUS: And did he have a blest demise, all free from
                       pain?

MESSENGER: It was extraordinary, most marvelous.
    You yourself saw how he went:

unled by friends but walking on and show-
ing us the way.
And when he'd reached that yawning orifice
where steps of brass sink rooted winding
down,
he stopped by one of the many branching
ways
close to that cup of rock where Theseus is
remembered
for his everlasting pact with Peiritheus.
And there he stood halfway between
that basin and the slab of Thoricus
by the old wild pear tree's hollowed trunk.
Then sitting down undid his squalid dress,
and calling for his daughters bade them
fetch
water to wash with from a spring
and some to pour in ritual for the dead.

So they went to Demeter's hill in front of
them—
that goddess of unfolding spring—
and soon had done all their father had
enjoined;
then bathed and tended him and dressed
him fittingly.
And when he was content that all was done,
with nothing further he could wish,
a grumbling sound of thunder came
from God's underworld.
It shook the girls with trembling and they
fell
weeping at their father's knees;
nor would they stop but beat their breasts
and sobbed.

And when he heard this bitter burst of grief,
he took them in his arms and said:
'This day, my daughters,
you shall have no father left to you.

≪≪≪≪≪≪≪≪≪≪≪≪≪≪≪≪≪≪≪≪≪≪≪≪≪≪≪≪≪≪≪≪≪

For all my life is done;
 your double burden of me done.
It was not easy, children, *that* I know,
 and yet one little word can change all
          pain:
 that word is LOVE; and love you've had
         from me
more than any man can ever give.
But, now you must live on—
 when I am gone.'

So did the three of them cling to one another,
 calling out and crying,
until at last they came to the end of tears
and sobs gave out and all was still.
Then in that stillness suddenly a voice was
         heard,
 terrifying; and their hair stood up with
         fear.
The voice of God it was, calling out and
         calling:
 'Oedipus, Oedipus, why do we delay?
You stay too long—too long you stay.'

And when he knew it was the voice of God
         that called,
 he craved King Theseus to draw near,
 and when he had he said to him:
 'Dear friend, put out your hand,
 my children put yours here—
now swear you'll never willingly abandon
         them
but wisely further all their needs
 as friendship and the time will tell.'
And Theseus, noble that he was, restrained
         his tears
and swore to keep his promise to his friend.

And the moment this was done,
 Oedipus, groping for his daughters, said:
 'Sweet children, now be brave, be good,

>>>>>>>>>>>>>>>>>>>>>>>>>>>>>>>>>>>>>>>

and leave this place.
Do not ask to see
   what you should not see
   and hear what you should not hear.
But go at once.
Only Theseus has the right to stay,
   and see what now unfolds.'

Such was his conversation;
   we heard it all of us.
And, sobbing with the girls, we left.
But after a little while, some paces off,
   we glanced around
   and Oedipus was nowhere to be seen
   but only the King,
   holding up his hands to screen his eyes
   as if he had beheld a vision
   too dazzling for a mortal's sight.
Then presently we saw him hail the earth
                    and sky
   in one great prayer.

                     [MESSENGER *pauses*]

How Oedipus has passed away no man shall
                    ever tell—
   no man but Theseus.
For in that hour no whitehot thunderbolt
               from God came down,
   no surge of giant sea to take him.
Some emissary perhaps from heaven came,
   or was the adamantine floor of the dead
   gently reft for him with love?
The passing of the man was pangless
   with no trace of pain nor any loud regret;
   it was of human exits the most marvelous.

But if you think I'm talking wild,
   wild talk will never woo belief.

CHORUS: But where are the girls and their escort now?

MESSENGER: Not far from here:
the sound of sobbing plainly tells they
come.

[ANTIGONE *and* ISMENE *slowly walk
into view*]

CHORAL DIALOGUE
[*which lasts till the end of the play*]

Strophe I

ANTIGONE: Cry, cry and cry again
Our cause is too complete
Two sisters and their sire.
Tears for their spellbound blood.
We lived his long-drawn life of pain
Until this dazing hour,
This passing and this vision.

CHORUS: What took place?

ANTIGONE: We can only guess.

CHORUS: He is gone?

ANTIGONE: Gone as you would wish it.
How else? No bloody war, no deep sea
caught him up,
but he was rapt to the land of no horizons
by some swift unseen design.
A night like death has blanketed our joy.
In distant lands, on a drifting sea,
how shall we live our bitter living?

ISMENE: I do not know.
Come bury me you halls of death
and lay me by my revered father's side.
So should I miss that life unlivable to come.

CHORUS: You loyalest of earth's daughters,
bear what God has brought you.
Let the fires of grief go out.
You were not wronged.

Antistrophe I

ANTIGONE: Ah! What was pain was joy
What lacked all love was love
When I had him in my arms.
O Father, Father, friend,
Clothed with perpetual gloom
In that deep territory
Not even there shall love
Hers and mine
Be barred from you.

CHORUS: He is content?

ANTIGONE: He had his wish.

CHORUS: His wish?

ANTIGONE: He wished to die on foreign soil
—he did:
his bed beneath the vaults of everlasting
shade,
his aftermath of mourning rich in tears.
O Father, yes, I cannot staunch their flow—
it is a flood of sorrow.
To die on foreign soil, you wanted that,
but—ah!—so far from me, forlorn!

ISMENE: Alas, dear sister, what remains for you and
me
with father gone forever?

CHORUS: Dear children, stop your tears—
he made a blessed end.
Misfortune quickly catches men.

Strophe II

ANTIGONE: Dearest, let's go back.

ISMENE: Whatever for?

ANTIGONE: I'm gripped by sudden longing.

ISMENE: What?

ANTIGONE: To see
his hidden home.

ISMENE: Whose home?

ANTIGONE: Poor Father's.

ISMENE: No, it cannot be. . . . And also, don't you
see . . . ?

ANTIGONE: Why this reproof?

ISMENE: Never did he have . . .

ANTIGONE: Go on.

ISMENE: . . . a tomb,
but died away from all of us.

ANTIGONE: Then take me there and kill me too.

ISMENE: What! leave me helpless and deserted?
Where should I lead my hopeless life alone?

Antistrophe II

CHORUS: Courage, children, courage!

ISMENE: Yes, but where
where is left to go?

CHORUS: There is a place.

ISMENE: But where?

CHORUS: Here: nothing shall molest you.

ISMENE: I know.

CHORUS: Then what?

ISMENE: Then how can we go
home?

CHORUS: You must not try.

ISMENE: But we are stricken.

CHORUS: You always were.

ISMENE: Yes, desperation once
        and now despair.

CHORUS: Great as the sea!

ISMENE: O Zeus
        what fate, what hope can urge us—and
                                what use?

[THESEUS enters with his escort]

THESEUS: Weep no more, sweet maidens.
        Where death has dealt so kindly
            there is no room for sorrow
            or nemesis will follow.

ANTIGONE: Good son of Aegeus, we beg you . . .

THESEUS: Daughters, for what favor?

ANTIGONE: Let these our eyes regard
            our father's place of resting.

THESEUS: That may not be.

ANTIGONE: But, lord, King of Athens—why?

THESEUS: Because, dear children,
            he himself has charged me
            not to let a single being
            approach these precincts
            or invade with prayers and voices
            his sanctuary of quiet.
        And if I keep this covenant, he told me,
            I keep my country free from harm.
        The god's ear heard these pledges,
            and God's eye, God of treaties,
            always seeing, saw it.

ANTIGONE: Then if his will and wish be this,
            enough for us. So be it.
        But send us back to Thebes,
            old Thebes so lost in legend.
        There shall we stem (if stemming be)
            the coming bloodbath of our brothers.

THESEUS: Why, so I shall.
                 I must not spare a pain to please
                 you and him, the dead, so lately seized.

CHORUS: Come then cease your crying.
             Keep tears from overflowing.
                 All's ordained—past all denying.

Antigone

>>>

for CLARISSA
δόμων ἄγαλμα

THE CHARACTERS

ANTIGONE: daughter of Oedipus and sister of Polyneices and Eteocles

ISMENE: sister of Antigone

CHORUS: citizens of Thebes

CREON: king of Thebes

A SENTRY

HAEMON: son of Creon and betrothed to Antigone

TIRESIAS: a blind prophet

A MESSENGER

EURYDICE: wife of Creon

A SECOND MESSENGER

TIME AND SETTING

After the death of OEDIPUS, *his two sons contend for the throne of Thebes.* POLYNEICES, *leading the Seven Champions, attacks from Argos and batters at the seven gates of Thebes.* ETEOCLES *defends the city, supported by* CREON, *who appears to have been acting as regent. In a great battle the two brothers meet face to face and kill each other. The Argive forces retreat. It is the morning after the battle. The dead still lie on the field, including* POLYNEICES *and* ETEOCLES. CREON, *once again the undisputed master of Thebes, proclaims that* POLYNEICES, *because he died fighting against his own city, shall be left to rot on the battlefield—the most ignominious of ends for any Greek.* ANTIGONE, *caught in a conflict of loyalties, to her dead brother and to the State, decides to defy* CREON's *edict. It is daybreak. She calls her sister out from the palace.*

Antigone

>>

PROLOGUE

ANTIGONE: Come, Ismene, my own dear sister, come!
What more do you think could Zeus require
of us
To load the curse that's on the House of
Oedipus?
There is no sorrow left, no single shame,
No pain, no tragedy, which does not hound
Us, you and me, towards our end.
And now,
What's this promulgation which they say
Our General's lately made to all the state?
Do you know? Have you heard? Or are you
sheltered
From the news that deals a deathblow to our
friends?

ISMENE: I've heard no news of friends, Antigone,
Good or bad, ever since we two were stripped
Of two brothers in a single day,
Each dismissing each by each other's hand.
And since the Argive army fled last night,
I've heard no more—either glad or sad.

ANTIGONE: That's what I thought. That's why I've
brought you here
Beyond the gates that you may hear my news
Alone.

ISMENE: What mischief are you hinting at?

ANTIGONE: I think you know: our two dear brothers.
Creon
Is burying one to desecrate the other.

165

‹‹‹

Eteocles, they say, he has dispatched
With proper rites as one judged fit to pass
In glory to the shades. But Polyneices,
Killed as piteously, an interdict
Forbids that anyone should bury him
Or even mourn. He must be left, unwept,
Unsepulchered—a vulture's prize, which rich
And rare is sweetly scented from afar.

Such is the purport of good Creon's news
For you and me, yes me; and now he's
                                        coming here
To publish it and make it plain. And anyone
Who disobeys will pay no trifling penalty
But die by stoning in the city walls.
There's your chance to prove your caliber,
Or else a sad degeneracy.

ISMENE: You firebrand!
Could I do a thing to change the situation
As it is?

ANTIGONE: You could. Are you willing
To share danger and suffering and——

ISMENE: Danger? What are you scheming at?

ANTIGONE: ——Take this hand of mine to bury the dead?

ISMENE: What! Bury him and flout the interdict?

ANTIGONE: He is my brother still, and yours—though you
Would have it otherwise. But I shall not
Abandon him.

ISMENE: What! Challenge Creon to his face?

ANTIGONE: He has no right to tamper with what's mine.

ISMENE: Sister, please, please! Remember how
Our father died: hated, in disgrace,
Wrapped in horror of himself, his own
Hand stabbing out his sight. And how
His mother-wife in one twisted off
Her earthly days with cord. And thirdly how
Our two brothers in a single day
Each achieved for each a suicidal
Nemesis.

And now, we two are left.
Think how much worse our end will be than all
The rest, if we defy our sovereign's edict
And his power. Remind ourselves that we
Are women, and as such not made to fight
With men. For might unfortunately is right
And makes us bow to things like this and worse.

Therefore shall I beg the saints below
To judge me leniently as one who kneeled
To force. I bend before authority.
It does not do to meddle.

ANTIGONE: I will not press you any more. I would
Not want you as a partner if you asked.
Go to what you please. I go to bury him.
How sweet to die in such pursuit! to rest
Loved by him whom I have loved,
Sinner of a holy sin, with longer time
To charm the dead than those who live. For I
Shall abide forever there.
So go
And please your fantasy and call
It wicked what the gods call good.

ISMENE: You know I don't do that. I'm just too weak
To war against the state.

ANTIGONE: Make your apologies! I go
To raise a tomb above my dearest brother.

ISMENE: Poor girl! And now you frighten me.

ANTIGONE: Don't fear for me. Be anxious for yourself.

ISMENE: At least tell no one what you do, but keep
It dark, and I shall keep it secret too.

ANTIGONE: Oh tell it, tell it, shout it out! I'll hate
Your silence more than if you told the world.

ISMENE: So fiery! In a business that chills?

ANTIGONE: Perhaps. But I am doing what I must.

ISMENE: Yes, more than must. And you are doomed to fail.

ANTIGONE: Why then, I'll fail, but not give up before.

ISMENE: Don't plunge into such a hopeless enterprise.

ANTIGONE: Urge me so, and I shall hate you soon.
The dead will justly hate you too.
Say that I'm mad, and madly let me risk
The worst that I can suffer and the best:
A death which martyrdom can render blest.

ISMENE: Go then, if you must, toward your end—
Fool, wonderful fool, and loyal friend.

[ISMENE *watches her sister walk away.*
She then goes into the palace]

[*The* CHORUS *enters and sings a song of triumph,*
celebrating the victory of Thebes over Argos]

ODE OF ENTRANCE

Strophe I

CHORUS: Sunshaft of the sun
Most resplendent sun
That ever shone on Thebes
The Seven Gates of Thebes:
Epiphany you broke
Eye of the golden day:
Marching over Dirce's streams
At dawn to drive in headlong flight
The warrior who came with shields
All fulminant as snow
In Argive stand at arms
Scattered now before the lancing sun.

LEADER: Propelled against our land
By Polyneices' claims
This screaming eagle circled round,
Caparisoned with arms he swooped,
His wings their shields of snow. His crest
Their helmets in the sun.

Antistrophe I

CHORUS: He stooped above our towers
Gaped above our gates,

His hungry spears hovered.
Then before he gorged
And glutted on our blood,
Before Hephaestus with his pitch
And flame had seized our crown of towers,
All the din that Ares loves
Was rended round his rear
And panic turned his flank.
The fight came on—a dragon-breathing foe.

LEADER:
The braggart's pompous tongue
Is hated most by Zeus
And seeing them advance superb
In clank of gold he struck their first
Man down with fire before he bawled
Triumph from the walls.

Strophe II

CHORUS:
Swung down in swift reverse
This lunatic in haste
Who came to breathe out fire
And hurricanes of hate:
Fell in a flaming arc
His brandished torch all quenched.
Great Ares like a war horse wheeled,
Ubiquitous his bounding strength,
Our helper in the field
Trampling in the dust
Havoc that he dealt with several dooms.

LEADER:
Seven champions dueled
With seven at the Seven
Gates and gave their panoplies
To Zeus, save two, the fatal two
Who sharing parents shared their fall,
Brother killing brother.

Antistrophe II

CHORUS:
But now that the triumph
The loudest of triumphs

‹‹‹

O joy-bearing triumph
Has come to our Thebes the city of chariots,
proud;

Why now let us chase
The memory far
Away of the wars that are past.
Come call on the gods
With song and with dance
All through the night at the temples,
And Bacchus shall lead
The round with his shouts
Shaking all Thebes with his revels.

LEADER: But look who comes, the lucky
Son of Menoeceus:
The man the gods have made our king.
What new vicissitudes of state
Do vex him now? Why has he sent
A herald to our summons?

FIRST EPISODE

[CREON *has entered from the palace.*
He addresses the CHORUS]

CREON: Gentlemen, the gods have graciously
Steadied again our ship of state, which storms
Have terribly tossed. And now I've called
you here
Privately, because of course I know
Your loyalty to all the House of Laius.
How again, when Oedipus was king,
Your duty never faltered. When he fell
You still upheld his sons.

But now that they
Have gone (sharing their double end upon
A single day—mutual murder, mutual
Recompense), I, nearest in line,
Enjoy the scepter and the throne.

Now, of course, there is no way to tell

The character and mettle of a man
Until you see him govern. Nevertheless,
I am the kind of man who can't and never
                                    could
Abide the tongue-tied ruler who through
                                    fear
Is shy of sound advice. I find
Intolerable the man who puts his country
Second to his friend.
                    For instance, if
I saw—and God's my witness—danger head-
                                    ing
For the state, I would speak out. I could
Not bear to make my country's enemy
My private friend. For, knowing as I do
Our country is the ship that bears us safe,
There *are* no friends aboard who sabotage.
So there you have my principles by which
I govern. In accord with them I made
The proclamation that you heard just now:
Eteocles, who died in arms for Thebes,
Shall have a glorious funeral, as befits
A hero going to join the noble dead.
But his brother Polyneices, he
Who came from exile breathing fire against
The city of his fathers and its shrines,
The man who came all thirsting for his
                                    country's
Blood, to drag the rest of us away
As slaves—I've sent the edict out that none
Shall bury him or even mourn. He must
Be left all ghastly where he fell, a corpse
For dogs to maul and vultures pick his bones.
You see the kind of man I am! You'll not
Catch me putting traitors up on pedestals
Beside the loyal man. I'll honor him
Alone, alive or dead, who honors Thebes.

LEADER: Your disposition is quite clear,
         Son of Menoeceus, Creon,

<<<<<<<<<<<<<<<<<<<<<<<<<<<<<<<<<<<<<<<<<<<<<<<<

Touching friend and enemy of this our city.
We know you have the power, too,
To wreak your will upon the living and the dead.

CREON: Then see to it that my injunctions are performed.

LEADER: Put the burden on some younger man.

CREON: No. Sentries are already posted on the corpse.

LEADER: Then what exactly do you want us to do?

CREON: Merely see there're no infringements of the law.

LEADER: No lunatic is going to welcome death.

CREON: And death it is. But greed of gain
Can often make men fools.

[A SENTRY *enters and walks hesitantly
towards the King*]

SENTRY: King. I won't pretend I come at breakneck speed,
All out of breath. I kept on stopping in my tracks
To think, and turning back. I held committee meetings
With myself: "You fool," I said, "you're heading straight
For the lion's mouth," or: "Blockhead, what're you waiting for?
If Creon gets the news from someone else, you're done!"
And so I come scurrying at a snail's pace down this short
Path which now is long, the 'forward' voice in charge.
And here I am: to tell a tale which makes no sense—
Which anyhow I'll tell. Because I do believe
Nothing bad can happen that isn't on one's ticket.

CREON: Come to the point. What's all the fuss about?

SENTRY: Now wait—let me brief you first—
I didn't do it—never saw who did.
It isn't right that I should take the blame.

CREON: Shoot your arrow, man! Don't hedge about.
You must have something very odd to say.

SENTRY: You know bad news improves if kept a little.*

CREON: Get on with it, I say, and go.

SENTRY: Well, I'll tell you: the body—someone's just
Buried it and gone. After sprinkling dust
On it and done the other pious things.

CREON: What do you mean? Who would have dared?

SENTRY: Don't ask me, sir! There's not a trace of pick
Or mattock. All the ground is baked, un-
broken,
No rut of wheels or sign of human hands.
When the sentry of the morning watch
Pointed to it—there it was at dawn:
The corpse, a horrid mystery, all veiled,
Not buried, lightly veiled with ritual dust
Its obsequies. No scavenger of prey,
No night marauding dog had left its mark.

Then recriminations flew:
Guard denouncing guard, until the lot of us
Came near to blows. There was no evidence
To clinch the fight or pin the blame on any-
one.
Nobody would confess. So nobody was crim-
inal,
And everyone was innocent
And called upon the gods and challenged
everyone
To handle redhot irons and walk through fire
To prove he neither did, connived at, knew,
This perpetrated deed.

Well, one of us

* Or, more strictly according to the Greek: "Well, unpleasant news is very unpleasant, you know!"

At last cut through the deadlock, saying:
              "Creon
Must be told." Which made us bend our
              heads
And stare. We could not contradict, yet knew
That one of us must go and tell him. Which
Is me. We cast the dice—and here I am—
Unwelcome and unwilling, and a most
Unhappy messenger of hapless news.

LEADER: Sire, I had misgivings from the first
That this was more than purely natural work.

CREON: Enough! You make me furious with such
              senile
Doddering remarks. Insufferable!
You really think they care 'two hoots,' the
              gods,
About this corpse? Next you'll say they make
It a priority to bury him in state
And thank him for his burning down their
              altars,
Sacking shrines, scouting laws, and raping
All the land—as if the gods were out
To compliment the bad. What utter non-
              sense!

No, far from this, the culprits are
A group of grumblers in the town, who from
The first opposed my edict, and in secret
Wagged their stiffnecked heads against my
              yoke.
These have led astray my guards with bribes.

Ah! Money! money is a currency that's rank,
Money levels cities to the ground,
Seduces men away from happy homes,
Corrupts the honest heart to shifty ways,
Makes men crooked connoisseurs of vice.

But all these hirelings, every one of them,
Will pay the price he's bargained for. I swear
It by almighty Zeus. And if you fail

edict like Oedipus

To find the man who did this burial,
And stand him here before my eyes,
Hades shall not receive your soul until
First you've hanged upon a cross and told
Me everything.

        That perhaps will teach
You where to look for profit, and that gold
Can glister from an evil source. Ah, money
Never makes as many as it mars!

SENTRY: Sir, may I have another word? Or do I go?

CREON: Can't you see your very voice distresses me?

SENTRY: In the ear or in the conscience?

CREON: What business is it of yours to analyze me?

SENTRY: Because my voice only hurts your ear.
Your conscience is affected by the deed.

CREON: By God, what a born chatterbox!

SENTRY: Maybe, but I didn't do the deed.

CREON: No, you just sold yourself for silver.

SENTRY: Oh! What can one do when even right reason
                         reasons wrong?

CREON: A logic-chopper and a wit! All right,
But don't imagine *that* will save your skin,
If you fail to stand the man before my face
You'll find that cheating does not pay.

            [CREON *strides into the palace*]

SENTRY: Well, let's hope he's found. But caught or not
(And only chance can tell), you won't find
                          me
Coming back again. My late miraculous
Escape still takes my breath away. I owe
The gods unbounded gratitude.

[*The* CHORUS *sings an ode which celebrates the
glory and prowess of man, as well as envisaging
his downfall should he prove either impious or
lawless* *]

* In other words, both Creon's and Antigone's fate is foreshad-
owed.

FIRST CHORAL ODE

Strophe I

CHORUS:

Creation is a marvel
And man its masterpiece:
He scuds before the southern wind
Between the loud white-piling swell.
He drives his thoroughbreds
Through Earth (perpetual
Great goddess inexhaustible)
Exhausting her each year.

Antistrophe I

The light-balanced light-headed birds
He snares; wild beasts according to their
kind.
In his nets the deep sea fish are caught—
O master mind of Man!
The free forest animal he herds,
The roaming upland deer.
The shaggy horse he breaks to yoke
The mountain-powered bull.

Strophe II

He's trained his agile thoughts
(Volatile as air)
To civilizing words.
He's roofed against the sky
The javelin crystal frosts
The arrow-lancing rains.
All fertile in resource
He's provident for all
(Not beaten by disease)
All but death, and death—
He never cures.

Antistrophe II

Beyond imagining he's wise
Through labyrinthine ways both good and
bad:
Distinguished in his city when
He is law-abiding, pious;
But displaced when he promotes
Unsavory ambition.
And then, I want no part with him,
No parcel of his thoughts.

SECOND EPISODE

[SENTRY *returns leading* ANTIGONE]

LEADER: What visitation do I see from heaven?
          And one I wish I could deny.
          I am amazed—it is Antigone.
          What! They bring you here in charge?
          Poor Antigone, daughter of unlucky Oedipus.
          Were you rash enough to cross the King?
          And did they take you in your folly?

SENTRY: Here she is, the culprit—caught redhanded
          in the act
          Of burying him. But where is Creon?

LEADER: Coming from the house, and just in time.

                              [*Enter* CREON]

CREON: Just in time for what?

SENTRY: Majesty, it's most unwise, I find,
          Ever to promise not to do a thing.
          Our second thoughts undo our first. Now look
          At me: I could have sworn I'd not
          Come scurrying back, after being almost
          Skinned alive by all your flailing threats.
          Yet here I am forsworn, and bring this girl,
          And all because I'm drunk with glad surprise
          (Yes, rushing to my head like wine)
          At having caught her at her obsequies.

<<<<<<<<<<<<<<<<<<<<<<<<<<<<<<<<<<<<<<<<<<<

    No throwing dice this time. Ah no!
    The lucky prize is absolutely mine.
    So take her, King. She's yours.
    Try her, judge her, as you want.
    But *I* expect to be dismissed at once,
    Cleared entirely of this tiresome affair.

CREON: Tell me first where and how you found her.

SENTRY: She was burying the man. Now you know.

CREON: Is this true? Are you serious?

SENTRY: I tell you I saw her burying the forbidden
                               corpse.
    Is that plain?

CREON: But how actually was she surprised and
                                 taken?

SENTRY: Well, it was like this:
    After we had returned to the spot (your most
    Unpleasant menaces still ringing in our ears),
    We dusted the earth from off the body
    And laid it bare. It was all soft and clammy.
    Then we sat on the brow of the hill to wind-
                                 ward
    Of the stench, and kept each other ready,
    Up to the mark, with threats on anyone
    Who nodded.
                 So we watched until the round
    And blazing sun began to scorch, now half-
    Way in his heaven. Then, quite suddenly,
    A whirlwind swept across the plain and hid
    The sky with choking dust, and stripped the
                                woods.
    We had to shut our eyes to bear its virulence.

    When at last it cleared, there stood
    The vision of this girl: her poignant cries
    Came sharp and bitter as a bird's that finds
    Its nest all pillaged and its fledglings gone.

    So was her shock, her execrations, sobs,
    When she saw the body bared. And then,

Immediately, she scoops up earth and sprin-
kles it.
Then, holding high a shapely brazen urn,
Pours three libations out, to celebrate the
dead.

We swooped at sight and closed upon our
quarry.
She did not flinch. And when we charged her
With her past and present crimes, she did not
contradict.

It made me glad and sad: relief for my escape
Yet some distress to see a friend in trouble.
When all's said and done, however,
The safety of one's own sweet skin comes
first.

CREON: Come girl, you with downcast eyes—do you
Plead innocent or guilty to these things?

ANTIGONE: Guilty. I deny not a thing.

CREON: You sir, you can go,
Scot-free of all these serious imputations.

Now, tell me, Antigone, as briefly as you can,
Did you know an edict had forbidden this?

ANTIGONE: Of course I knew. Was it not publicly proclaimed?

CREON: So you chose flagrantly to disobey my law?

ANTIGONE: Naturally! Since Zeus never promulgated
Such a law. Nor will you find
That Justice publishes such laws to man be-
low.
I never thought your edicts had such force
They nullified the laws of heaven, which,
Unwritten, not proclaimed, can boast
A currency that everlastingly is valid;
An origin beyond the birth of man.
And I, whom no man's frown can frighten,
Am far from risking Heaven's frown by
flouting these.

‹‹

I need no trumpeter from you to tell me
I must die. We all die anyway.
And if this hurries me to death before my
                                    time—
Why, such a death is gain. Yes, surely gain
To one so overwhelmed with trouble.

Therefore, I can go to meet my end
Without a trace of pain. But had I left
The body of my mother's son unburied
Where he lay—ah! that would hurt. For this,
I feel no twinges of regret. And if
You think I am a fool, perhaps it is
Because a fool is judge.

LEADER: My word! The daughter is as headstrong as
                                    the father.
            Submission is a thing she's never learnt.

CREON: You wait and see! The toughest will is first
            To break: like hard untempered steel,
            Which snaps and shivers at a touch when
                                    fresh
            From off the forge.
                              And I have sometimes
                                    seen
            High-mettled horses curbed by just the bit.

            One who is my neighbor's slave
            Can ill afford to put on airs. And yet,
            This girl, already versed in disrespect
            When first she disobeyed my law, now adds
            A second insult—vaunts it to my face.
            O, she's the man, not I, if she can walk
            Away unscathed! I swear I hardly care
            If she be my sister's child, or linked
            To me by blood more closely than
            Any member of my hearth and home—
            She and her sister will not now escape
            The direst penalty. I say the sister too.
            I charge her as accomplice of this burial.
            Call her forth. I saw her whimpering

In there just now, all gone to pieces. So
Does remorse blurt out the secret sin.
And yet, I think the opposite is worse:
Crime detected, glorifying crime.

ANTIGONE: Is there something more you want? Or just
my life?

CREON: Not a thing, by God! It gives me what I want.

ANTIGONE: Why dawdle, then? Your conversation is
Hardly something I enjoy, or could;
Nor mine be more acceptable to you.
And yet, it ought to be: where could I win
Respect and praise more validly than this—
Burial of my brother?

Not a man
Here would deny it, if his tongue
Were not locked in fear. Unfortunately
Dictatorship (blessed in so much else be-
sides)
Can lay the law down any way it wants.

CREON: Your view is hardly shared by all these Thebans here.

ANTIGONE: They think as I, but trim their tongues to you.

CREON: Are you not ashamed to differ from such
men?

ANTIGONE: There is no shame to reverence relatives.

CREON: And the other duelist who died—was he no
relative?

ANTIGONE: He was. And of the same father and same
mother.

CREON: So, slighting one, you would salute the other?

ANTIGONE: The dead man would not agree with you on
this.

CREON: Surely! If you make the hero co-honored
with the blackguard.

ANTIGONE: It was his brother, not his slave, that died.

CREON: Yes, and ravaging our land,
While *he* fell as its champion.

‹‹

ANTIGONE: Hades makes no distinction in its rites and
honors.

CREON: The just and unjust do not urge an equal
claim.

ANTIGONE: The crime (who knows?) may be called a
virtue there!

CREON: Not even death can metamorphose hate to
love.

ANTIGONE: No, nor decompose a love to hate.

CREON: Curse you! Find the outlet for your love
down there.
No woman while I live shall govern me.

[ISMENE *is brought in under guard*]

LEADER: See where Ismene comes
Crying from the palace gates,
Her face all flushed.
A sister's tears are breaking rains,
Upon her cheeks and from her eyes—
Her loveliness a shadow.

CREON: Come, you serpent—secret lurker in my
home,
Who sucked my blood even while I nurtured
You two sister vipers at my throne—
Speak. Confess your part in burying him.
Or do you dare abjure complicity?

ISMENE: I did it too. If she'll allow my claim.
I share with her the credit and the blame.

ANTIGONE: That is not true. You did not share with me,
Nor did I grant you partnership.

ISMENE: But now that your poor ship is buffeted,
I'm not ashamed to sail the voyage at your
side.

ANTIGONE: The dead of Hades know whose act it was.
I do not take to those who take to talk.

ISMENE: Sister, do not scorn me; let me share
Your death and holy homage to the dead.

ANTIGONE: No share in work, no share in death. And I
Must consummate alone what I began.

ISMENE: Then what is left of life to me when you are
gone?

ANTIGONE: Ask Creon. You and he are friends.

ISMENE: Ah! Must you jeer at me? It does not help.

ANTIGONE: You are right. It is a joyless jeering.

ISMENE: Tell me, even now: how can I help?

ANTIGONE: Save yourself. I shall not envy you.

ISMENE: Poor dear sister—let me suffer with you!

ANTIGONE: No. For you choose life, and I chose death.

ISMENE: When all my protests were of no avail.

ANTIGONE: We played our different parts, with different
applause.

ISMENE: And also shared an equal shower of blame.

ANTIGONE: Look up! You live! And I died long ago—
When I dedicated life to serve the dead.

CREON: These girls, I swear, are crazed: one mad by
birth,
The other by attainment.

ISMENE: Yes, my lord, for when misfortune comes,
He sends our reason packing out of doors.

CREON: And yours went flying fast, the moment you
Chose to have your portion with the damned.

ISMENE: Yet, with her gone, what portion had I left?

CREON: Do not mention her. She does not still exist.

ISMENE: You would even kill your own son's bride?

CREON: Let him sow his seed in other fields.

ISMENE: A match like theirs will *not* repeat itself.

CREON: I shudder at the jades who court our sons.

ANTIGONE: My darling Haemon—how your father heaps
disgrace on you!

CREON: Silence! I've heard enough of you and your
accursed marriage.

LEADER: You would not really tear your own son's
                                    bride from him?

CREON: Let us say that *death* is going to come be-
                                    tween.

LEADER: I fear, I fear, it's fixed. Her death is sealed.

CREON: Yes, by you and me.
                            Servants,
            Off with them and lock them up.
            No more roaming. They are women now.
            The breath of Hades pressing close to kill
            Can make the bravest turn, and turn the
                                    bravest will.

[*The* CHORUS *begins an ode which rings omi-
nously for the House of Oedipus*]

SECOND CHORAL ODE

Strophe I

CHORUS: Happy the man who has not sipped
            The bitter day;
            Whose house is firm against divine assault.
            No planted curse
            Can creep on generations like the dark and
                                    driven surge
            Which, pounded from the bosom of the sea
                                    by Thracian winds,
            Churns perpetually the ooze in waves that
                                    throw
            Down upon the headlands swept and carded
                                    by the storm—
            Its thunderous mass.

Antistrophe I

LEADER: So do I see the House of Labdacus struck
                                    down:
            In all its generations victimized by some
            Pursuing deity. Its useless dead. And now,

At last, the sun gone down in blood. The final
                                          hope
Of Oedipus put out in smoke in Hades dust—
The fruit of recklessness and pride.

Strophe II

CHORUS: O Zeus, what creature pits himself against
                                          thy power?
         Not sleep, encumbrous with his subtle net:
         And not the tireless moon.
         Thou in ancient splendors still art young
         When worlds are old—
         On Mount Olympus.

LEADER: Let Ambition touch his wings on many flow-
                                             ers;
         Blessed to one he comes—as hope;
         All ruin to another
         Lured to fly too high,
         His life too late hot ashes now beneath his
                                              feet.

Antistrophe II

CHORUS: For Wisdom and a sage said long ago:
                 "If evil good appear
                 To any, fate is near.*
                 Unscathed he'll blithely go
                 Then pride will bring him low."

THIRD EPISODE

LEADER: Look, here Haemon comes, your youngest
                                            son,
         Driven perhaps by pangs of grief for her
         His sentenced bride—a bitter, thwarted bride-
                                            groom.

CREON: We shall see in a moment, and without the
                                      need of seers.

* I have borrowed the rendition of this couplet (so exactly right)
from Ronald Storr's translation in the Loeb Classical Library.

Son, do you come provoked against your
father
For the death warrant of your would-be
bride,
Or still my loving son, whatever I may do?

HAEMON: Father, I am your loving son, and you the
wise
Preceptor of my ways, whom I must follow.
No marriage I could make would ever match
The good of your abiding counsel.

CREON: Well
Spoken son! A son's first study is
Unremitting deference to his father's will.
Such is a parent's prayer: to see grow up
A race of filial sons to deck his home,
Who hate those *he* hates, give his friends
The selfsame honor that the father gives.
But he who rears a brood of worthless sons,
What can one say of him but that he breeds
Troubles for himself and gossip for
The ill-disposed.

And so, my son, you must
Not lose your balance for a woman's sake,
You must not hug a joy that's cheap, and
cools—
An evil woman for your bed and board.
No wound is worse than counterfeited love.
She is your evil genius, throw her out
And let her go and find a mate in Hades.
She alone from all the city stands
Convicted of rebellion.

I will not
Be made to break my word to Thebes. She
dies.
So let her plead to Zeus the sanctity
Of kindred ties.

How can I, if I nurse
Sedition in my house, not foster it

Outside? And if a man can keep his home
In hand, he proves his competence to keep
The state.

          But one who breaks the laws and
                     flouts
Authority, I never will allow.
For, whom the state appoints to govern, *he*
Must be listened to in little things,
In just things, in things their opposite.
And I am confident that one who thus
Obeys, would make a perfect subject or
A perfect king; who even in the thick
Of flying spears will not desert his post
But staunchly stands at his comrade's side.

O Anarchy! there is no greater curse
Than anarchy. It topples cities down,
It crumbles homes. It shatters allied ranks
In broken flight, which discipline kept
                    whole—
For discipline preserves and orders well.

Let us then defend authority
And not be ousted by a girl. If yield
We must, then better yield to man, than have
It said that we were worsted by a woman.

LEADER: What you say (unless my wits have run
To seed) appears to me to make good sense.

HAEMON: Father:
Reason is God's greatest gift to man.
I would not dream of criticizing yours.
But other men can reason rightly too.
As your son, you see, I find myself
Marking every word and act and comment
Of the crowd, to gauge the temper
Of the simple citizen, who dares not risk
Your scowl to freely speak his mind.

                    But I
From the shadows hear them: hear
A whole city's sympathy towards

This girl, because no woman ever faced
So unreasonable, so cruel a death
For such a generous act:
                                        She would not
                                             leave
Her brother lying on the battlefield
For carrion birds and dogs to maul.
                                        "Should not
Her name be writ in gold?" they say. And so
The whisper grows.
                                        You know, my father,
                                             how I prize
Your happiness. For, sons and fathers crown
Each other's glory with each other's fame.
Then, don't entrench yourself in your opinion
As if everyone else were wrong. The kind of
                                             man
Who always thinks that he is right, that his
Opinions, his pronouncements, are the final
                                             word,
When once exposed shows nothing there.
But a wise man has much to learn without
A loss of dignity. He must not strain.

See the trees in floodtime, how they bend
Along the torrent's course, and how their
                                             twigs
And branches do not snap, but stubborn trees
Are torn up roots and all. In sailing too,
When fresh weather blows, a skipper who
Will not slacken sail turns turtle—
Finishes his voyage beam-ends up.

So let your anger cool, and change your
                                             mind.
I may be young but not without some sense.
Let men be wise by instinct if they can,
But when this fails be wise by good advice.

LEADER: Sire, you should listen if he speaks
                 Judiciously.

And you sir, too. You both
Have spoken to the point.

CREON: You mean that men of my years have to learn
To think by taking notes from men of his?

HAEMON: In nothing that's not just. It is my
Merit not my years that count.

CREON: Your merit is to foment lawlessness.

HAEMON: You know I do not plead for criminals.

CREON: So this damsel here is not a criminal?

HAEMON: The whole of Thebes says 'no.'

CREON: And I must let the mob dictate my policy?

HAEMON: See who now is speaking like a boy?

CREON: Do *I* rule this state, or someone else?

HAEMON: A one-man state is no state at all.

CREON: The state is his who rules it. Is that plain?

HAEMON: The state that you should rule would be a
desert.

CREON: This boy is obviously in league with the girl.

HAEMON: I'm in league with you. Are you a woman?

CREON: You reprobate! At open loggerheads with
your father!

HAEMON: On the contrary: you at loggerheads with
open justice!

CREON: Oh? My sin, of course, the discharge of my
rights?

HAEMON: What rights—when you trample on the rights
of God?

CREON: Insolent pup! A woman's lackey!

HAEMON: Lackey to nothing of which I am ashamed.

CREON: Not ashamed to speak up for that troll?

HAEMON: I speak for you, for me and for the gods
below.

CREON: You shall not marry her alive.

HAEMON:	Well then, dead—one death beckoning to another.
CREON:	You threaten me?
HAEMON:	One cannot threaten empty air!
CREON:	You shall regret dispensing wisdom which you ill could spare!
HAEMON:	If you were not my father I'd say you were perverse.
CREON:	You lady-help—don't come toadying to me!
HAEMON:	All right then: make remarks and never listen to an answer!
CREON:	You'd tell me that? By Heaven, wait, you shall
	Not rant and jeer at me without your chastisement.
	Off with the wretched girl, I say she dies
	In front of him, before her bridegroom's eyes.
HAEMON:	She shall not die—don't think it—by my side.
	And you shall never see my face again.
	I commit you raving to your chosen friends.

[HAEMON *rushes out*]

LEADER:	Gone—Your Majesty! The man has gone!
	He is young, his grief will make him desperate.
CREON:	Let him dare—O let him dream up acts
	As superhuman as a fiend's. These girls,
	He shall not snatch from death.
LEADER:	You do not mean to kill them both?
CREON:	You are right. Not the one who did not meddle.
LEADER:	What kind of death do you plan?
CREON:	I'll take her down a path untrod by man
	I'll hide her living in rock-hewn vault,
	With ritual food enough to clear the taint
	Of murder from the City's name.
	I'll leave her pleading to her favorite god—

Hades. He may charm her out a way to life.
Or perhaps she'll learn though late the cost
Of homage to the dead is: labor lost.

[CREON *walks away into the palace*]

[*The* CHORUS *sings an ode to the power of love,
which can unman our better judgment*]

THIRD CHORAL ODE

Strophe

CHORUS:　　Love untamed
Lighting on largess
With spoils
All night upon a maiden's cheek
You roam the seas
Pervade the hills
And in a shepherd's hut you lie.
Shadowing immortal gods
You dog ephemeral man:
Madness your possession.

Antistrophe

You infect all common sense
You sting us to this strife
Of kinsman fighting kin.
The bride has but to glance
To win with your lyrical light
A place among the Laws.
When Aphrodite laughs
You win, O Love!

FOURTH EPISODE

[ANTIGONE *is led in, guarded*]

LEADER:　　And now you turn on me
Unman my loyalty
Unloose my tears to see

<<<<<<<<<<<<<<<<<<<<<<<<<<<<<<<<<<<<<<<<

Antigone
Pass her wedding bower
Death's chamber, pass
So easily.

Strophe I

[ANTIGONE *and the* CHORUS *chant alternately*]

ANTIGONE: See me friends and citizens,
Look on this last walk—
The sun's light snuffed out with my dower.
                                    And death

Leading me to Acheron
Alive, where all must sleep.
No wedding march, no bridal song
Can cheer my way,
Whom Hades Lord of the dark lake weds.

CHORUS: Yet you walk with fame
Bedecked in praise towards
The deadman's cave.
No sickness severed you
No sword incited struck;
All mistress of your fate
You move alive, unique,
To Hades Halls.

Antistrophe I

ANTIGONE: Oh but I have heard
What happened to that Phrygian girl
Poor foreigner the child of Tantalus,
Who clings in stone,
Captured, petrified,
Like ivy on the heights of Sipylus;
Where all the rains, they say, the flying snow
Weather her wasting form which weeps
In waterfalls. I feel her trance,
Her lonely exodus, in mine.

CHORUS: And she a goddess born of gods,
While we are mortals born of men.

What greater glory for a woman's end
To partner gods in death
Who partnered gods in life!

Strophe II

ANTIGONE: Ah! Now you laugh at me.
Thebes, Thebes, by all our father's gods—
You my own proud chariot city—
Can you not wait till I am gone?
And you sweet Dirce's streams and Theban
groves,
At least be witnesses to me with love
Who walk in dismal passage to my heavy
tomb;
Unwept, unjustly judged,
Displaced from every home,
Disowned by both the living and the dead.

CHORUS: Perhaps you aimed too high
You dashed your foot on fate
Where Justice sits enthroned.
You fell a plummet fall
To pay a father's sin.

Antistrophe II

ANTIGONE: You touch my wounds, my memories, make
fresh
Again my tears, my father's threefold curse
Brought on the blighted House of Labdacus
That horrid bridal bed—
My bastard origin;
My fated mother sleeping with her son
To father me in incest.

Parents, here I come,
Home at last; not wed,
No broken spell.

Brother, when you blindly made your match
You made your death, despoiling me of life.

CHORUS: Pious is as pious does.
            Where might is right
            There is no right.
            You walked to death with open eyes.

                        Epode

ANTIGONE: No one at my side
            No one to regret,
            Uncelebrated love
            Is all I have for my last walk. And you
            Eye of the blessed sun—
            I shall miss you soon.
            No tears will mourn me dead. No friend to
                                                    cry.

                                        [CREON *enters*]

CREON: Listen you!
            Panegyrics and dirges go on forever
            If given the chance. Dispatch her at once, I
                                                    say.

            Seal up the tomb.
            Let her choose a death at leisure, or
            Perhaps an underground life forlorn.
            We wash our hands of this girl
            Except to take her from the light.

ANTIGONE: Come tomb, my wedding chamber come,
            You sealed-off habitations of the grave!
            My many family dead, finished, fetched
            In final muster to Persephone.
            I am last to come, and lost the most of all.
            My life still in my hands. And yet I come
            (I hope I come) towards a father's love,
            Beloved by my mother; and by you
            My darling brother—loved.
                                    Yes, all of you,
            Whom these my hands have washed, pre-
                                        pared and sped
            With ritual to your burials. And now,
            Sweet Polyneices, dressing you, I've earned

This recompense, though richly honored you
The just will say.

No husband dead and gone,
No children lisping 'mother' ever could
Have forced me to withstand the city to its
face.
On what principles do I assert so much?
Just this:

A husband dead, another can be
found;
A child, replaced; but once a brother's lost
(Mother and father dead and buried too)
No other brother can be born or grows again.
That's my principle, which Creon stigmatized
As criminal—my principle for honoring
You my dearest brother.

So taken,
So am I led away: a spinster still,
Uncelebrated, barren and bereft of joys;
No children to my name. An outcast stripped
Of sympathy I go alive towards
These sepulchers of death.

What ordinance,
What law of heaven broken? What god left
For such as me to cast my eyes towards?
And whom address, when sacraments must
now
Be castigized as sacrilege?

And if these things are smiled upon by
heaven,
Why, when I'm dead I'll know I sinned.
But if I find the sin was theirs—God spare
Them retribution much more terrible
That what they now unjustly heap on me.

LEADER: See how she goes headlong driven
By the capricious gusts of her own spirit!

CREON: Putting to disgrace her loitering guards. Who
shall pay for it.

ANTIGONE: There is death in that remark: the sound of
                                                            death.

LEADER: And by no hope or euphemy of mine
              Can otherwise your finish be described.

ANTIGONE: Ah, Thebes!
              I am going now going,
              Divine ancestral Thebes!
              Cast but a glance
              Your princes' eyes
              Towards this royal remnant—me.
              See my martyrdom,
              See its origin:
              Piety to pity.

                              [ANTIGONE *is led away*]

[*To console* ANTIGONE, *the* CHORUS *recalls
other situations of fate similar to her own*]

FOURTH CHORAL ODE

Strophe I

CHORUS: Hidden from the sun
              Housed behind brass doors
              Danaë's beauty too was locked away
              Her nuptial cell a tomb
              And she, my child, yes she
              A royal daughter too:
              The rare receptacle of Zeus's golden seed.

LEADER: O Destiny, marked mysterious force!
              No mound of coins,
              No panoplies of war,
              No ramparts keep you out;
              And through the dark sea booming,
              No ship escapes.

Antistrophe I

CHORUS: The savage son of Dryas
              That Edonian king, was put in prison,

Sealed by Dionysus in a cavern,
For his jeering;
Where his bawling
Quietly faded into echoes;
Learned to know in final meekness
Bacchus whom his madness baited
When he quenched the mad Bacchantes
And offended all the muses of the flute.

Strophe II

LEADER: Then there is the nightmare story
Seen by Ares from the Euxine
Seashore: seen the bride of Phineus,
Jealous, maddened, stabbing sightless
Both his sons, to plunge the sharpness
Of her spindle in their eyes.
Seen their vacant plea for vengeance
Plead in pools of socket-bloody staring.

Antistrophe II

CHORUS: So they rotted, wrecked completely,
Wasting sorrow for their mother's
Stupid mating, which his noble
Birth from Erectheus could not
Save. And she a daughter cradled
By Boréas in the caverns,
In the tempests, lunging swiftly,
Bolting like a colt from heaven—
Shot precipitate above the hills.

LEADER: Look, Antigone, they had her,
Finally the Fates they struck her down.

FIFTH EPISODE

[*The blind prophet* TIRESIAS *is led in by a boy. His opening lines should be chanted*]

TIRESIAS: Theban rulers, here we come:
One pair of eyes, a double road,
And the blind man led by others.

<<<<<<<<<<<<<<<<<<<<<<<<<<<<<<<<<<<<<<<<<<

CREON: What news, old Tiresias?

TIRESIAS: I shall tell you. Listen to the prophet's words.

CREON: Have I ever failed to listen to your words?

TIRESIAS: Therefore have you safely piloted the state.

CREON: And gladly do I own my debt to you.

TIRESIAS: Then beware, you're standing once again
　　　　　　　　　　　　upon the razor's edge.

CREON: How so? Your words and aspect frighten me.

TIRESIAS: Listen, I'll read the signs and make it plain:
I was sitting in my ancient chair of augury
Where the birds all gather by the swamp,
When suddenly a noise not heard before
Assaults my ears: a panic screaming and
A pandemonium deafening jargon—beaks
And talons whirring, tearing; pattering
Of wings that shocked me as a portent.
At once I kindled sacrifice.
But Hephaestus fanned no leaping flame.
Instead a sort of sweat distilled from off the
　　　　　　　　　　　　thigh-fat,
Slid in smoke upon the sputtering fire.
The gallbladders burst and spurted up,
The grease oozed down and left the thigh-
　　　　　　　　　　　　bones bare.
These were the signs I learnt from off this
　　　　　　　　　　　　boy:
Omens from a ruined sacrifice.
He is my eyes as I am yours.

Yes, the city sickens, Creon;
These the symptoms, yours the cussedness
That caused them: Dogs and crows all glut-
　　　　　　　　　　　　ted carrying
Desecrated carrion to the hearths
And altars—carrion from the poor unburied
Son of Oedipus.
　　　　　　　　Burnt offerings go
Up in stench. The gods are dumb. The birds

Of omen cannot sing. But obscene vultures
Flap away with crops all gorged on human
flesh.

Think, son, think! To err is human, true,
And only he is cursed who having sinned
Will not repent, will not repair. He is
A fool, a proved and stubborn fool.
Give death
His due, and do not kick a corpse.
Where is renown to kill a dead man twice?

Believe me, I advise you well.
It should be easy to adopt advice
Which is entirely for your good estate.

CREON: Old man, you pot away at me like all
The rest, as if I were a bull's-eye. Now
You aim your seer-craft at me. Well, I'm sick
Of being bought and sold by all your sooth-
saying tribe.
Bargain away! The silver-gilt of Sardis,
All the gold of India, is not enough
To buy this man a grave. Not even if
Zeus's eagles come to fly away
With carrion morsels to their master's throne.
Even such a threat of such a taint
Will not win his body burial.
It takes much more than human remains
To desecrate the majesty of God.
Old Tiresias—
The most reverend fall from grace
When lies are sold wrapped up in honeyed
words.

TIRESIAS: Creon! Creon!
Is no one left who takes to heart that——

CREON: Come, let's have the platitude!

TIRESIAS: ——That prudence is the best of all our
wealth.

CREON: As folly is the worst of all our woes?

TIRESIAS: Yes, infectious folly! And you are sick with it.

CREON: I have no intention of encouraging a fish-
wife's set-to with a seer.

TIRESIAS: Which is what you do when you say I sell my
prophecies.

CREON: As prophets do—a money-grubbing race.

TIRESIAS: Or as kings, who grub for money in the dung.

CREON: You realize you are guilty of lese majesty?

TIRESIAS: Majesty? Yes, thanks to me you are king of
Thebes.

CREON: And you are not without your conjuring
tricks. But still a crook.

TIRESIAS: Go on! You will drive me to divulge something that—

CREON: Out with it! But not for money, please.

TIRESIAS: Unhappily for you this can't be bought.

CREON: Then don't expect to bargain with my wits.

TIRESIAS: All right then! Take it if you can.
                     A corpse
For a corpse the price, and flesh for flesh—
One of your own begotten. The sun shall not
Run his course for many days before you pay.
You plunged a child of light into the dark;
Entombed the living with the dead; the
                     dead—
Dismissed, unmourned, denied a grave, a
                     corpse
Unhallowed and defeated of his destiny
Below. Where neither you nor gods above
Must meddle you have thrust your thumbs.
                     Do not
Be surprised that heaven, yes—and hell,
Have set the Furies loose to lie in wait
For you—ah! ready with the punishments
You have engineered for others.
Does this sound like flattery for sale?
Yet a little while and you shall wake

To weeping and gnashing of teeth in the
house of Creon.
Insensate, they'll rise, those other cities,
Whose mangled sons received their obsequies
From dogs and prowling jackals; from
Some filthy vulture flapping to alight
Above their very hearths to bring them home,
Desecration reeking from its beak.

There! You asked, and I have shot my angry
arrows.
I aimed at your intemperate heart. I did not
miss.

Come, boy, take me home, and let him spew
His choler over younger men. He'll learn
A little modesty in time,
A little meekness soon.

[TIRESIAS *is led out by his boy*]

LEADER: *There's* fire and slaughter for you, King!
He has gone, but my gray hairs were long
since shining
Black, before he ever stirred the city
To a false alarm.

CREON: I know. You point the horns of my dilemma.
It's hard to eat my words, and harder still
To risk catastrophe through stubborn pride.

LEADER: Son of Menoeceus, be advised in time.

CREON: To do what? Speak and I shall listen.

LEADER: Go and free the damsel from her vault.
Then entomb the lonely body lying stark.

CREON: You advise that? You really think I must?

LEADER: Must, King, and quickly too. The gods,
Provoked, never wait to mow men down.

CREON: How it goes against the grain
To smother all one's heart's desire!
I cannot fight with destiny.

LEADER: Quickly, go and do it. Don't trust to others.

CREON: Yes, I go at once.
          Servants, servants—on the double.
          You there, fetch the rest. Bring axes all
          And hurry to the hill. My mind's made up.
          I'll not be slow to let her loose myself
          Who locked her in the tomb. To value life
          (O my regrets!), then one must value law.

              [CREON *and servants hasten away in
                                all directions*]

[*The* CHORUS *sings a desperate Paean to Bacchus begging him to come and save the stricken
city of Thebes and the House of Oedipus*]

PAEAN

Strophe I

CHORUS: We urge you by a hundred names
          O flower of Semele's wedding
          Son of Zeus and son of thunder
          Singer of sweet Italy:
          Call you Regent of the Revels
          In the copsy lap of Deo's glades,
          Call you Bacchus haunting Thebes
          (Mother of the Bacchanals)—
          By Ismenus's quicksilver stream
          Where the dragon's teeth are sown.

Antistrophe I

LEADER: Bacchus and your nymphs Bacchantes
          Dots of fire and wreathing torches
          By Castalia's springs, and mounting
          Smoke above the crested forks
          Call you coming from the hills of
          Nyssa, green with vineyards green like
          Ivy dripping to the shore.

Strophe II

CHORUS: Call you to your favorite city
          (City of your thunder-ravished

Mother) to a people dying—
City shadowed by the plague.
Come with gentle feet and save us,
Cross the crying straits, come quickly.
Hurry from Parnassus.

Antistrophe II

LEADER: Come you choreographer
Master of the pulsing stars
And voices of the night, O Prince
Appear! You Zeus begotten!

All your choric troop proceeding,
Midnight maenads in their frenzy,
Come, Iacchus, O come!

[*There is a long pause, while the strains of
the* CHORUS *die away. A* MESSENGER *enters*]

EPILOGUE

MESSENGER: Men of the House of Cadmus and of Am-
phion,
How rash it is to envy others or despair:
The luck we adulate in one today, tomorrow
is
Another's tragedy. There is no stable horo-
Scope for man.
Take Creon: he if anyone
I thought was enviable. He saved this land
from all
Our enemies, attained the pomp and circum-
stance
Of king—his children decked like olive
branches round
His throne. And now it is undone, undone!
And what
Is left is not called life but living death. His
wealth,

His kingly state, is nothing to him now, with
                                    gladness gone;
Vanity of vanities—the shadow of a shade.

LEADER: What further news do you bring of royal
                                    ruin?

MESSENGER: Death. The living guilty for the dead.

LEADER: Who is striking, who is stricken? Say.

MESSENGER: Haemon's gone. Blood spilt by suicide.

LEADER: Suicide? Or by his father's hand?

MESSENGER: Both. Driven to it by his father's murdering.

LEADER: O Prophet, your prophecy's come true!

MESSENGER: So stands the case. Draw your own conclu-
                                    sions.

LEADER: Look, Creon's queen, Eurydice,
Unhappily is here. Is it chance
Or has she heard the deathknell of her son?

[EURYDICE *staggers in supported by
                                    her maids*]

EURYDICE: Yes, good citizens, all of you, I heard,
Even as I went to supplicate
The goddess Pallas with my prayers. The
                                    gate
Was not unlocked before I fell fainting
At the sound of moaning that I heard.
I was stunned, my maidens bore me up.
But tell me everything however bad.
I am no stranger to the voice of sorrow.

MESSENGER: Sweet lady, I was there. I shall not try
To camouflage a detail of the truth.
For where is the point of comfort in a lie,
So soon found out? The truth is always best.

I went on foot with Creon to the plateau
                                    where
Polyneices lay abandoned still,
All mauled by dogs. And there we prayed
                                    the goddess

Of the Great Divide, and also begged
Pluto's mercy too.

> We sprinkled him
With holy water, lopped fresh branches down
And lit a fire to burn away his poor
Remains. We heaped a monument to him,
A mound of his native earth.

> > Then turned
away
To open up the vault in which there lay
A virgin waiting on a bed of stone
For her bridegroom—Death.

> > And one of us,
Ahead, heard voices like a deep despair
Echoed from that hideous place of honey-
moon.
He hurried back and told the King, who then
Drew near and seemed to recognize those
hollow
Sounds. He gave a bleat of fear:

> > "Oh, are
My heart's forebodings true? I cannot bear
To tread this path: my son's voice strikes my
ears.
Hurry, hurry, servants, to the tomb,
And through those stones once pried away
peer down
Into that cadaverous gap and tell
Me if it's Haemon's voice. Oh, tell
Me I am heavenly deceived!"
His panic sent us flying to the vault
And in the farthest corner we could see
Her hanging with a noose of linen round her
neck,
And leaning on her, hugging his poor lover
Lost to Hades, Haemon, bridegroom, broken,
Cursed the Father who had robbed him,
Pouring out his tears of sorrow.
Creon burst into a fit of crying

When he saw him; hurried to him sobbing:
"Poor misguided boy, what have you done?
What were you thinking of? And now?
Come to me, my son. Your father begs you."

But the boy stared at him with hatred,
Spat for answer in his face, and drew
A double-hilted sword and lunged towards
His father as he fled.

            Then, desperate,
He pressed against that sword and drove it
            home,
Halfway up the hilt into his side.
And conscious still, but failing, limply folded
Close Antigone into his arms—
Choking blood in crimson showers upon
Her waxen face.

            Corpse wrapped in love
With corpse he lies. Married not in life
But Hades. Lesson to the world that folly
Wreaks a havoc measureless to man.

[EURYDICE *retires, dazed, into the house*]

LEADER: What does her exit mean? The Mistress went
Silent, with no word of sadness or of comfort.

MESSENGER: I am troubled too. And yet I hope
The reason is she shrinks from public sorrow
For her son. And goes into the house
To lead her ladies in the family dirge.
She will not be unwise. She is discreet.

LEADER: You may be right. But I do not trust
Extremes of silence or of grief.

MESSENGER: Let me go into the house and see. Extremes
Of silence, as you say, are sinister:
Her heart is broken and can hide
Some dangerous design.

[MESSENGER *hurries out*]

[CREON, *half holding the body of* HAEMON,
which is carried on a bier, slowly approaches]

LEADER: Look, the King himself draws near; his load,
In a kind of muteness, crying out his sorrow
(Dare we say it?) from a madness of mis-
doing
Started by himself and by no other.

CREON: Purblind sin of mine!
There is no absolution
For perversity that dragged
A son to death:
Murdered son, father murdering.
Son, my son! Cut down, dead!
Poor life that's disappeared,
And by no youthful foolishness
But by my folly.

LEADER: Late, too late, your reason reasons right!

CREON: Yes, taught by bitterness.
Oh, some god has cast his spell,
Has hit me hard from heaven,
Let my cruelty grow rank;
Has slashed me down, my joys,
Trod me in the earth:
Man, man, oh how you suffer!

[*Enter* SECOND MESSENGER]

MESSENGER: Sire, you are laden,
You the author loading:
Half your sorrow in your hands,
The other half still in your house—
Soon to be unhidden.

CREON: What half horror coming?

MESSENGER: Your queen is dead:
Mother for her son;
The suicidal thrust;
Dead for whom she lived.

CREON: O! Hades, pitiless receiver!
Your mercy dwindles, does it?
Must you bring me words
That crush me utterly?

ᐊᐊᐊᐊᐊᐊᐊᐊᐊᐊᐊᐊᐊᐊᐊᐊᐊᐊᐊᐊᐊᐊᐊᐊᐊᐊᐊᐊᐊᐊᐊ

I was dead and still you killed me.
Slaughter was piled high;
Ah, then, do not tell me
You come to pile it higher:
A son dead, then a wife.

LEADER: Look, the doors are open—look!

[*The scene suddenly opens (by a movement of*
'εκκύκλημα * *) and discloses* EURYDICE *lying*
dead surrounded by her attendants]

CREON: Oh, oh, oh!
A second deathblow.
Fate, my bitter cup
Can have no second brimming,
Yet the sight I see laid out
Blasts a second sorrow.
My son just lifted up
A corpse; and now a corpse his mother.

MESSENGER: Her heart was shattered
And her hand drove keen the dagger.
At the altar, there she fell,
And darkness swamped her drooping
Eyes when cries of sorrow—
Sobbing for Megareus,
Long since nobly dead
Son—and for this other,
Mingled with her dying gasp
And curses on you—killer.

CREON: My heart is sick with fear.
Will no one lance
A two-edged sword
Through this bleeding seat of sorrow?

MESSENGER: She charged you rightly,
Yes, this lifeless thing:
You double filicidal killer!

* The 'εκκύκλημα (*ekkuklema*) was a theatrical machine which
could open up the stage to an inner scene—frequently a murder
or a suicide.

CREON: Tell me, how did she die?

MESSENGER: Self-stabbed to the heart;
Her son's death ringing
New dirges in her head.

CREON: God, this sin, my sin,
Can never be forgiven.
I killed her, I
Can own no alibi.
Take me quickly
Take me servants hence,
And let me be forgotten.

CHORUS: Good advice at last!
If anything be good.
In so much bad.
But badness needs good riddance.

CREON: Oh! let it come!
Let it appear!
Let it break!
My last and golden day:
Best, the last, the worst,
To rob me of tomorrow.

LEADER: Tomorrow is tomorrow.
Future cares have future cures,
And we must mind today.

CREON: All my prayer was that:
The prayer of my desires.

LEADER: Your prayers are done.
Man cannot flatter Fate,
And punishments must come.

CREON: Then lead me please away;
A rash weak foolish man—
A man of sorrows
Who killed you, son, so blindly
And you my wife—so blind.
Where can I look?
Where hope for help?

<<<<<<<<<<<<<<<<<<<<<<<<<<<<<<<<<<<<<<<<<<<<

When everything I touch
Is dust, and death
Has leapt upon my life.

LEADER: Where wisdom is, there happiness will crown
A piety that nothing will corrode.
But high and mighty words and ways
Are flogged to humbleness, till age,
Beaten to its knees, at last is wise.

Appendix

>>>

PRODUCTION AND ACTING

There are two main dangers in the production of a Greek play: one is to overplay the dignity; the other is not to be aware of that dignity at all. The first becomes a desperate and futile endeavor to recapture the externals of the Greek theater. It is arty and self-conscious and, in battening on period effects (we are being Greeks, boys and girls—is my mask on straight?), destroys the very humanity and timelessness it seeks to promote. The second, confusing the Greek idealization and simplification of human nature with unreality, and seeking to redress the balance, tries to turn the heroic figures of Aeschylus, Sophocles and Euripides into everyday nonentities. It attempts the prosaic, trivial, chatty, and obliterates the heights and depths of tragedy.

These are the two chief false principles. Occasionally they are blended and a third type of mistake is hatched, inheriting the artiness of one parent and the lack of restraint of the other. Professor J. T. Sheppard, the great Sophoclean scholar, well describes it in a production of *Oedipus the King* which he had the discomfort of witnessing: ". . . [the] actors, not altogether, I suspect, of their own free will, raged and fumed and ranted, rushing hither and thither with a violence of gesticulation which, in spite of all their effort, was eclipsed and rendered insignificant by the yet more violent rushes, screams, and contortions of a quite gratuitous crowd." (Introduction to *The Oedipus Tyrannus of Sophocles*, Cambridge, 1920.)

What then is the enlightened producer to aim for? Let him first of all remember that these plays were performed before enormous audiences, perhaps up to 30,000 people. Masks, costumes, spectacles, and the whole style of production (whatever its sacred origins) were designed for long-distance effect:* a purpose that no longer exists in our smaller and more intimate theater.

Secondly, this vast audience did not consist predominantly of sophisticated city dwellers but of honest-to-goodness people coming in from the country—many of them farmers and perhaps even (we cannot be certain) slaves. The point is that it was not a highbrow audience, even if it understood better than any modern audience the cultural framework of its own myths. It was not at all the kind of audience that came for culture or would tolerate any 'art for art's sake.' These people came to be thrilled and moved to tears. All the external apparatus of the Greek stage—song, dance, mime, masks and spectacle —was simply a means to creating a vivid arena wherein the great human emotions could be worked out in public. In some two thousand four hundred years these emotions have not changed. Only the external circumstances have changed. Oedipus, Jocasta, and Antigone were first of all human beings. The heart of Sophocles which beat to their passions was first of all a human heart—only incidentally Greek and of the fifth century B.C.

Thirdly, let both producer and actor remember that it is only through his words—by their very choice and sound —that Sophocles the poet achieves his power to move us. It is through the beauty, restraint, perfect adaptation of every tone and emphasis of the language to each situation, that he is able to sink us deeply into the pathos of his characters. Assuming that the translator has done his best to capture something of the original word-magic, let those words be heard. It is absolutely necessary that the poetry be read as poetry and not given a prose pointing. It is absolutely necessary that the lines are not deprived of their rich embodiment of rhythm and cadence. The poet has already done the work of establishing the neces-

---

* Masks not merely typed a character's predominant expression, but also helped to project the actor's voice.

sary tension and dramatic force. No amount of 'acting' can be a substitute for it. Let the voice be measured but natural; never 'tharsonic,' that blend of stage and pulpit which some actors affect when they come to poetry. If the lines are enunciated clearly and rhythmically, if the acting follows the poetry and is not imposed upon it, then the result will tend to be great acting. It will be the transparent window through which the characters—created by the words—are sincerely seen; idealistically human yet never falsely intimate.

As to the Chorus, let the producer keep in mind its purpose: to underline, develop, and if possible increase, the suspense built up by the dialogue. Certainly there can be music, mime, and dance, provided all this does not detract from the intelligibility of the words. The music should tend to build up background rather than to lead. It can be an ally to the force of the poetry if used sensitively and not as an end in itself. Woodwind and percussion instruments—flute and soft drum—would seem to be the most natural accompaniment to the Greek movement. They can be used to usher in and to usher out the main characters. The Sophoclean chorus numbered fifteen, but it can be raised to almost any number or lowered to as few as five. It is better for the chorus to speak its lines severally than to chant them in unison: though there may be occasions when a group answers a group.

The scenery should be simple and not distract the viewer's imagination by striving for realism. A drop curtain may be helpful, though the Greeks did not use one. An interval almost certainly destroys the accumulated tension. If masks are used they should not be replicas of the Greek mask, which was much larger than life.

These then are the principles. There are few rules, if many possibilities. Only that production of a Greek play will be valid which puts the human emotions first and enables the spectator to feel with and for its subjects. Let producer and actor resist the two falsifying temptations: the purely mundane, which can never be heroic, and the overstylized, which can never be human.

NOTES

(1) Note on Meter

The meter throughout the dialogue of this rendering of the Theban Plays is iambic, as it is in Sophocles. If to anyone's eye it reads too unvaryingly I can only counsel him to read it aloud, keeping to the natural stresses of the words. Dramatic speech automatically tends to create its own background of counterpoint rhythms. Indeed, the danger on the stage is not that poetry should sound monotonous but that it should not sound at all. Sophocles himself never loses his hold on an unmistakable 'beat' which should not be lost in the English even though English prosody is 'qualitative' rather than 'quantitative.' In either language it is the beauty of the measure itself that contributes to the depth, loftiness and intensity of the drama.

In the *Antigone* I keep to a more or less traditional blank versification, but in the other two plays I have made the attempt to tauten the metrical value of dramatic speech while at the same time rendering it more elastic and capacious. In *Oedipus the King* I have adopted a prosodical device which helps the line to follow the sense of the words more than it does in ordinary iambic pentameter. The lines lengthen and shorten as the need may be, but whether they stretch into hexameters or shrink into trimeters the over-all count of a passage remains iambic pentameter. I have called it 'Compensated Pentameter.' In *Oedipus at Colonus,* to match by some kind of prosodical analogy this last and supreme mastery of Sophocles over human speech, I have done away with even compensation and embark on a completely freewheeling iambic measure which I think (and hope) is proof against all misreading.

(2) Note on *Oedipus the King*

The power of *Oedipus the King* is cumulative. It opens slowly, weightily, and rises to a flood of emotion that nothing can stop. This initial solemnity—at times almost a stiffness—I have been at pains to keep in the English. It is a formal and hieratic quality and lasts till about line 86, the first exit of OEDIPUS. However, it must not be assumed that this 'grand manner' of utterance casts aside the already perceptible elements of pity, pathos, irony, fear, and suffering which come to such full fruition later.

(3) Note on Creon

It must not be thought that the character of CREON in *Oedipus the King* corresponds exactly to the CREON in the other two plays. The Theban Plays were not written at the same time nor conceived originally as a strict unity.

(4) Note on the Appearance of the Greek Script

For those who are interested, here are the first six lines of the *Antigone* written out in Greek lower case. If they are written out in capitals (as Greek often was) they will look like the lines at the beginning of this book. It is the same passage.

> ﹖Ω κοινὸν αὐτάδελφον ᾽Ισμήνης κάρα
> ἆρ᾽ ἆσθ᾽ ὅτι Ζεὺς τῶν ἀπ᾽ Οἰδίπου κακῶν
> ὁποῖον οὐχὶ νῶν ἔτι ζώσαιν τελεῖ,
> οὐδὲν γὰρ οὔτ᾽ ἀλγεινὸν οὔτ᾽ ἄτης ἄτερ
> οὔτ᾽ αἰσχρὸν οὔτ᾽ ἄτιμόν ἐσθ᾽ ὁποῖον οὐ
> τῶν σῶν τε καμῶν οὐκ ὄπωπ᾽ ἐγὼ κακῶν.

(5) Note on the Texts

The texts I have followed have in the main been those of Lewis Campbell, Oxford, 1879, and Richard Jebb, Cambridge, 1889–93. I support Campbell as against Jebb in not excising lines 904–12 of the *Antigone*. These lines seem to me to throw important light on ANTIGONE's character and motives.

GLOSSARY OF CLASSICAL NAMES

Abae: An Ancient town in the country of Phocis (northern Greece) which was famous for its temple and oracle of Apollo.

Acheron: A river of the lower world, round which the souls of the dead were said to hover.

Aidoneus: Another name for Hades—god of the Nether World.

Amphion: With his twin brother Zethus, Amphion marched against Thebes, killed Lycus the King (their cast-off mother's husband) and Dirce, who had become Lycus's wife. They tied Dirce to a bull which dragged her about until she was dead, then they threw her body into a fountain—hence 'Dirce's Fountain.' Hermes gave Amphion a lyre on which he played with such magic skill that the stones moved of their own accord and formed a great wall around Thebes.

Amphitrite: Wife of the god Poseidon and goddess of the sea. She was the mother of Triton.

Aphrodite: Goddess of love and beauty. The Roman Venus.

Apollo: The son of Zeus and Leto. He was the god of prophecy, of help and reward, and of punishment. He had more influence upon the Greeks than any other one god.

Areopagus: Criminal court of Athens—so called because it sat on the Hill of Ares, west of the Acropolis.

Ares: Bloodthirsty god of war. Roman Mars.

Argos: A city-state in the Peloponnesus. Also, a rival to Sparta.

Artemis: Twin sister of Apollo and goddess of the moon and of the hunt. She sent plagues and sudden deaths (especially to women), but she also cured and alleviated sufferings. She is the Roman Diana.

Athena: Or Athene—the Roman Minerva. Daughter of Zeus and Metis (Zeus swallowed her mother before her birth and Athena sprang from his head—dressed in full armor and shouting a mighty war cry). Goddess of power and wisdom; Athena was the preserver of the state and maintained law and order. She is said to have created the olive tree and invented the plow.

Attica: A division of Greece in which Athens was the principal city.

Bacchus: Earlier called Dionysus. Greek and Roman god of wine and revelry.

Bacchanal: Religious revelry centered round the god Bacchus.

Bacchae: Priestesses of Dionysus who by wine and mad enthusiasm worked themselves to a frenzy at the Dionysiac festivals.

Boreas: God of the North Wind. In the Persian War he helped the Athenians by destroying the ships of the barbarians.

Cadmus: Son of Agenor, king of Phoenicia, and also the brother of Europa. He founded Thebes by killing a dragon sacred to Ares and then on the advice of Athena sowing its teeth. Armed men sprang up from the ground who fought and killed one another till only five remained. These five then helped Cadmus to build the city of Thebes.

Castalia: A fountain on Mount Parnassus sacred to Apollo.

Cephisus: The largest stream in Attica.

Cerberus: The three-headed dog which guarded the entrance of Hades Halls.

Cithaeron: A lofty mountain range separating Boeotia from Megaris and Attica. It was sacred to Dionysus.

Corybantes: The attendants of the Phrygian goddess Cybele, who followed her through the night with dancing and revelry.

Cronus: Youngest of the Titans—son of Uranus (heaven) and Ge or Gaea (earth). He was father, by Rhea, of Hestia, Demeter, Hera, Hades, Poseidon, and Zeus. He ousted Uranus from divine supremacy and in turn was dethroned by Zeus. He is the Roman Saturn.

Cyllene: The highest mountain in the Peloponnesus.

Danaë: She was locked in a brazen tower by her father because an oracle said her son would grow to kill its grandfather. In her tower Zeus visited her in a shower of gold, and thus impregnated she gave birth to Perseus—who years later accidentally killed his grandfather with a discus.

Daulia: An ancient town in Phocis.

Delos: The smallest of the Cyclades islands. As it was the birthplace of Apollo and Artemis, Delos became the holy seat of the worship of Apollo and the site of a famous temple.

Delphi: A small town in Phocis, but the most celebrated in Greece because of its oracle of Apollo.

Demeter: Sister of Zeus, goddess of earth, protectress of agriculture and all the fruits of the earth. She became identified with the Roman Ceres.

Dionysus: God of wine and the god of tragic art and protector of the theater. The Roman Bacchus.

Dirce: See Amphion.

Dragon's Seed: The armed men that sprang up from the teeth of the dragon which Cadmus slew. They fought and killed one another except five, who became the ancestors of the Thebans.

Dryas: Father of the Thracian king, Lycurgus.

Dryads: Nymphs of the woods (female divinities of the lower order).

Edonia: A part of Thrace where the people were celebrated for their orgiastic worship of Bacchus.

Eleusis: A town of Attica, northwest of Athens, which had a magnificent temple of Demeter, and gave its name to the great festival and mysteries of the Eleusinia, which were celebrated in honor of Persephone and Demeter.

Erectheus: (Erichthonius)—son of Hephaestus. Athena reared him without the other gods' knowing. He became king of Athens and is said to have introduced the worship of Athena there.

Eumenides: The 'Kindly Ones' (which is a euphemism for the Furies or Erinyes, dreaded daughters of Earth and Night). They were usually represented as winged maidens with serpents entwined in their hair and blood dripping from their eyes. They dwelt in the depths of Tartarus. They punished men both in this world and after death—usually for disobedience towards parents, disrespect of old age, perjury, murder, violation of laws of hospitality, and improper conduct towards suppliants.

Euxine: The Black Sea.

Furies: See Eumenides.

Hades: See Aidoneus.

Helicon: Range of mountains in Boeotia which are covered in snow most of the year. They were sacred to Apollo and the Muses. From Helicon sprang the famous fountains of the Muses.

Helios: God of the sun who sees and hears everything.

Hephaestus: God of fire and the forge, who made Achilles' shield. Son of Zeus and Hera. The Roman Vulcan.

Hermes: The Roman Mercury. Usually depicted wearing winged shoes and hat and carrying the caduceus in his hand. He was the herald and messenger of the gods and also invented the lyre. He conducted the shades of the dead from the upper to the lower world.

Iacchus: The solemn name of Bacchus in the Eleusinian mysteries.

Io: Beloved by Zeus and hated by Hera, who turned her into a heifer. Hera tormented her with a gadfly. In a con-

≪≪≪≪≪≪≪≪≪≪≪≪≪≪≪≪≪≪≪≪≪≪≪≪≪≪≪≪≪≪≪≪≪≪≪≪≪≪

stant state of frenzy, she fled from land to land until she at last found rest on the banks of the Nile and returned to her original form.

Ismenus: A small river in Boeotia, the stream Dirce flowed into.

Ister: The river Danube, flowing to the Black Sea through the land of the Scythians.

Isthmian: The Isthmian games were held once a year on the Isthmus of Corinth.

Lyceus: A surname of Apollo, who was worshipped in Lycia, a small district in South Asia Minor.

Maenads: Another name for the Bacchantes, meaning 'to be mad,' because they were frenzied in their worship of Bacchus.

Mars: Roman name for Ares, god of war.

Megareus: A son of Eurydice, wife of Creon.

Mercury: Roman name for Hermes.

Nemesis: The goddess who measured out happiness and misery, visiting suffering and losses on those who were too fortunate. She became known as the divinity who punished the criminal.

Niobe: The daughter of Tantalus and wife of Amphion, king of Thebes. She boasted of the number of her children, thus annoying Apollo and Artemis, who slew all her children. Zeus turned the weeping mother into a stone on Mount Sipylus in Lydia, which during the summer always shed tears.

Nymphs: Minor goddesses of nature, haunting rivers (Naiads), woods and trees (Dryads and Hamadryads), mountains (Oreads), and seas (Nereids).

Nyssa: The legendary scene of the nurture of Dionysus. It came to mean several places sacred to Dionysus.

Oea: A deme (small district) in Attica belonging to the Oenean tribe.

Olympus: The highest of the range of mountains separating Macedonia and Thessaly. It was the home of Zeus and all his dynasty.

Pallas: A surname of Athena.

Pan: A son of Hermes. The god of shepherds and flocks. He loved music and invented the syrinx or shepherds' flute. He led the nymphs in dance, but, as he had the legs and horns of a goat and dwelt in the forests, travelers were frightened of him.

Parnassus: A mountain range in southern Greece: usually signifying the highest part, which is a few miles north of Delphi. It was the seat of Apollo and the muses, and sacred to Dionysus.

Peiritheus: A hero in Attic history who gave his name to a deme (one of the hundred townships into which Attica was divided).

Peloponnesus: Southern peninsula of Greece, connected with Hellas by the isthmus of Corinth. It contained the powerful city-states of Sparta and Argos.

Pelops: Meaning the Peloponnesus, which was named after Pelops, son of Tantalus, who came to Elis and brought with him such riches that the whole peninsula was named for him.

Persephone: Daughter of Zeus and Demeter and wife of Hades, therefore Queen of the Dead. The Roman Proserpine.

Phasis: A river of Colchis in Asia Minor from whose banks the pheasant is said to have come.

Phineus: Who blinded his own sons because of alleged treachery. The gods punished him in turn with blindness and sent the Harpies to torment him. The sons of Boreas eventually freed him from the monsters.

Phoebus: 'Bright' or 'Pure'—an epithet of Apollo.

Phrygia: A country in Asia Minor, probably settled by Thracians.

◄◄◄

Pluto: Another name for Hades—used as a euphemism by those who were frightened to mention Hades.

Poseidon: God of the Mediterranean. Brother of Zeus and Hades, who rode his chariot over the waves and lived in a palace in the depths of the sea. The Roman Neptune.

Prometheus: A god who stole fire from heaven and taught the mortals its use, and many arts. He was chained to a rock and submitted to the perpetual torture of an eagle's eating away his liver (and Zeus's healing it each night so that the eagle could begin again). Hercules eventually freed him.

Pythia: A priestess of Delphi, who, after exhaling the intoxicating vapors which rose from the ground in the center of the temple, uttered the revelations of Apollo.

Pytho: The ancient name of Delphi.

Rhea: Mother of Zeus, Poseidon, Hades, Hera, Demeter, Hestia. "Mother of the Gods," who was wildly and often orgiastically worshipped through the whole of Greece.

Sardis: An ancient city of Asia Minor which contained the palace and the rich treasury of the Lydian kings.

Semele: The daughter of Theban Cadmus who was beloved by Zeus. Jealous Hera tricked her into asking Zeus to visit her as god of thunder. He warned Semele of the danger but nevertheless complied. She was killed by lightning but Zeus saved her child, Dionysus, whom she had just conceived by Zeus (as thunder). Dionysus later carried her from the underworld to Olympus and she became immortal.

Sipylus. See Niobe.

Sphinx: "The Strangler," a winged monster with a lion's body and the head and breasts of a woman. She took up her station on a rock outside Thebes and proposed a riddle to every passer-by, strangling those who could not answer. When Oedipus solved the riddle she flung herself from her rock and perished.

Tantalus: A wealthy, worldly king, and son of Zeus. After his death Zeus punished him in the underworld by eternal thirst and hunger. He placed him in a lake, which receded from him each time he tried to drink, and beneath branches of fruit which Tantalus could never quite reach.

Tartarus: A name synonymous with Hades. Also a place as far below Hades as Heaven is above the earth.

Thebes: The chief city of Boeotia; said to have been founded by the hero Cadmus. The walls of the city were built by Amphion and his brother Zethus. Legend had it that when Amphion played his lyre, the stones themselves moved into place to form the wall.

Thoricus: A hero in Attic history who gave his name to a deme (one of the hundred townships into which Attica was divided).

Thrace: A Greek city-state which was inhabited by rapacious and warlike people.

Titans: Giant deities, the primordial children of Heaven and Earth, who were overthrown and succeeded by Zeus and the Olympian gods.

Zeus: The Roman Jupiter: greatest, most powerful, and ruler of all the Olympian gods. The husband of Hera, the Roman Juno.

Acknowledgments

To the following professors and associate professors of Classical Languages for their criticism, suggestions, comments and encouragement:
Mr. Bernard N. W. Knox of Yale University
Mr. Martin Ostwald of Columbia University
Miss Helen Bacon of Smith College
Mr. John A. Moore of Amherst College
To Miss Siobhan McKenna for enthusiastically reading the first draft of the *Antigone*.
To Mr. Carl Beier for producing selections of the *Antigone* on the C.B.S. program "Look Up and Live."
To Miss Jacqueline Brookes and Miss Janine Claire for giving moving performances in the C.B.S. production.
To Professor John Sweeney for recording the *Antigone* at the Lamont Library, Harvard University.
To Professors of English, Daniel Aaron and Edna Williams, Smith College, for their encouragement once when I needed it.
To Mr. Martin Wilbur Tanner and to Mr. Leonard Baskin, Assistant Professor of Art, Smith College, for advice on typography.
To Mr. Jack Barrett and Miss Vaun Gillmor for arranging readings of the *Antigone* and for their constant interest.
To the Trustees of the Bollingen Foundation for their generous award to enable me to continue my work on translating Greek drama.
To Dr. William Carlos Williams for his enthusiasm from the beginning.
To my mother-in-law, Mrs. Martin Wilbur Tanner, for patiently putting up with me in her house and garden, doing what was all 'Greek' to her.
Lastly, and most of all, to Mr. Victor Weybright.